INNOCENCE DESIRED

INNOCENCE DESIRED

BRENDA BACON

INNOCENCE DESIRED

iUniverse books may be ordered through booksellers or by contacting:

iUniverse
1663 Liberty Drive
Bloomington, IN 47403
www.iuniverse.com
844-349-9409

ISBN: 978-1-6632-5505-1 (sc)
ISBN: 978-1-6632-5506-8 (e)

Library of Congress Control Number: 2023913936

Print information available on the last page.

iUniverse rev. date: 08/01/2023

Dedicated to those who believed in me and the dream.
I am blessed every day to have you in my circle.

CHAPTER 1

Billy, Darius, Jolene and I strolled across the warm Hawaiian beach. The waves roared in the background as a soft, gentle wind kissed our faces. This was paradise. I took in a deep breath, sighing in peace. Gorman picked me up in his arms and spun me around while our lips locked in passion.

"Well, isn't that just too sweet?", a voice snarled. From a balcony overlooking the beach was a pair of binoculars focused in on our foursome. The man snorted in disgust at the sight of us.

"I've got them in the sights of my rifle. Give me the order and they're good as dead. Come on, just say the word, boss. I'll take them all down right now."

"No, you fool, I need the girls alive." Trent Winter lowered the binoculars slowly. Pursing his lips and eyes growing cold, he sneered, "I have something much worse in mind for them."

I sat down in the warm sand and stretched out on a towel. The sun warmed my skin. Jolene had music playing softly from her phone. Darius eyed the scantily clad beauties and Jolene smacked him playfully on the arm. Billy was on the phone, checking in on the casino. Even now, he was working. That casino was his pride and joy; and it was his. The smell of the salt air filled my senses. Children playing and laughing in the distance at the water's edge. I closed my eyes and soaked in the sounds. I breathed out slowly, relaxing. Light gave way to the dark.

"Give my that fucking disk, or I'm gonna splatter your brains all over the sand and bury your ass right here!"

Trent Winter's voice boomed over me, thunder and storm clouds above me. My eyes snapped open, a gun barrel inches from my face. Lightning struck the beach within feet from me. The beach was empty except for Winter and me. He cocked the 45 and pressed it into my forehead. "Now you're dealing with me!" I blinked in disbelief. "Time's up- your dead!" he shouted in rage. The deafening sound of the bullet escaping the chamber and penetrating my skull, combined with a thunderclap that shook the entire beach.

I jumped to my feet and screamed. Ripping my sunglasses off of my face and throwing them to the ground, I gasped. I began scanning my surroundings feverishly. Light filled my senses as the storm clouds and Trent Winter faded away.

Billy snared my arm. "Jasmine, Jasmine," he whispered, "shoosh, it's ok. You're just dreaming. You're ok. We're right here."

My eyes were wild, my heart racing. Between panicked gasps, I exploded, "He's here! He's watching us!"

Gorman hugged me tightly, trying to calm the hysteria that had overcome me. Jolene turned off the radio. On lookers stared. Barrington addressed the others around us, "Just a bad dream, folks. Everything's alright. Sometimes she suffers from nightmares. Nothing to see here." People shook their heads sadly and went about their business.

"He's here, Billy," I flooded breathless. "He's here somewhere."

Billy whispered softly, "Baby, he's not here. Nobody's here. Nobody knew we were coming here. It was just a bad dream honey, that's all. Calm down. We're here – me, Darius, Jolene. Just a bad dream." He stroked my hair gently, finally releasing me from his grip.

My eyes frantically searched the beach. I scanned the shoreline in terror. "No," I said with hollow disbelief. "I can feel him, Billy. He's here. He's watching us."

2

"Ken Parks is dead," Gorman sighed in an aggravated tone. "Stop it, Jasmine. Just stop it," he demanded. Jolene and Barrington moved in close to console my hysteria.

A bead of sweat ran down my temple. My heart was racing, my hands trembling. Jolene added, "It's going to be ok, sis. We're fine- just a bad dream like Billy said. It's all good."

Darius and I gazed into each other's eyes. I pleaded desperately in silence for somebody to believe me. Barrington looked up and down the beach several times, looking for anything out of the ordinary. He shook his head from side to side, indicating he did not feel a threat.

My line of sight scanned the luxury high rise hotels in the distance. He could be in any of those. A room on the top floor or even a roof top. In ghostly breath, I whispered, "He _is_ here. I can feel him."

"Jasmine, stop this nonsense. It was only a frigging dream," Gorman spat. "I'm getting you therapy when we get back home."

"So now I'm crazy," I growled, snapping up the towel and walking away.

Back at the rooftop, Trent Winter's henchman lowered his binoculars slowly. "Boss, what the hell was that?", he barked. "She looked right at us. This broad a witch or psychic, or something? It's like she knew we were here. How's that possible? And what was all that chaos?"

Trent seemed puzzled as well, shrugging in shock. "She felt us, Sal. This is going to take a skill you're lacking."

"Yeah? What's that boss?"

"Finesse. Planning. Surprise. We can't go about this Ken Parks style- rushing in, guns blazing. That's it. Pack it up. We're going back to New York."

As I stomped through the sand in anger, Jolene ran and caught up to me. "Men," she hissed. "Such assholes. Do you really think he's here?" My sister gulped in terror, now out of ear shot of Gorman and Barrington. Instantly, the men were at our side.

Darius, always the diplomat announced, "So, I'm getting hungry. Who's down for some food?" I walked on in silence. I wasn't some kind of crazy person, and it sure didn't feel like a dream. Even though he knew I was furious at him, Billy put his arm around my shoulder and kissed me on the top of the head for emotional support.

As we entered the hotel, Darius's phone began ringing. He answered with a grin, but sudden deep lines appeared on his forehead. He became hushed, sullen. "Bad news, Billy." Our group stopped in our tracks to hear his announcement.

Billy questioned, "So what is it?"

"Trent Winter picked his new enforcer."

"And?", the boss interrogated, on edge.

"Sal Aguzzi."

Billy rubbed his face with the palm of his hand, closing his eyes, and sighing, "Why am I not surprised?"

"Who is that?", my sister quizzed.

Barrington replied, "We'll brief you when we get back home. We're on vacation. We'll worry about that later." Billy and Darius locked eyes, deep concern shared silently between them.

As soon as the plane touched down in Las Vegas, Gorman turned to Darius and ordered in a hushed tone, "Call an emergency security meeting. I want everyone on deck in 15 minutes. Conference center at the casino. We can't go home until you brief everyone on Winter's new acquisition."

Darius held out his hands. "Billy, I don't have anything prepared. We don't even have a photo of him."

"Now," Gorman said softly. "There's no time for fancy speeches. Just tell us what you know."

Barrington put his hands on his hips and sighed loudly. Billy shot him a hard glance. "Ok, just don't expect much, boss."

"We're not going home yet?", Jolene questioned, confused by the sudden development.

Gorman and Barrington were already on their phones, summoning the top leaders. My sister stared at them feverishly at work.

I closed my eyes and whispered to her, "This is bad."

We drove to the casino in silence. To my amazement the conference room already had a dozen men inside. Some faces I knew; like the head of security for the casino and night club Billy owned. Roderick sat at the long table. I wondered what he was doing there. I guessed he had been called to take Jolene and myself home. Billy never included us in his briefings with his underlings before.

The eyes about the table shifted side to side nervously. What was this unexpected beckoning? They knew something big was about to go down. I stood back, wringing my hands in silence. Shuffling my feet, I gathered the courage to address Billy. "Boss, you want us to go down to the casino floor and wait for you? I can see this important to you."

Barrington ran his fingers through his hair. "We're all here."

Jolene took two steps towards the exit.

"No!", Gorman's voice boomed. "You two – at the table." My sister gazed at him in confusion. "Sit, both of you." We quickly took our seats. I was uncomfortable; feeling awkward- like a child that just moved from the kiddie table to the big people's table for Thanksgiving dinner. My hands were trembling. The air was thick with tension, sucking my breath from my lungs. I hadn't been scared like this since being captured by Ken Parks. My heartbeat pounded in my temples with a shallow breath of fear. The room fell silent in apprehension.

Billy stood at the head of the conference room table, placing his fingertips on the desktop. "I want to thank you all for coming on such short notice. I know Darius told you that this is an emergency security briefing. We have just found out who Trent Winter has chosen as his second in command."

"Who?", Roderick demanded forcefully. I turned my head to glare at his boldness in this situation. How the hell did a mere butler get invited to sit at this table? Not one other eye turned to challenge him. My mouth flopped open in shock and my sister kicked my shin under the table.

Darius sneered through clenched teeth. "Sal Aguzzi." There were groans from some, cursing from others. Roderick leaned back in his chair, a long, loud breath of air escaping his lips.

Barrington continued, "I know some of you have probably heard his name mentioned from time to time. We're here to fill in those who don't know him on a few details. You'll have to bear with me. I have no formal brief prepared, but I'll give you what I can and hope to add more as we go."

"He's elusive. No photos have ever been taken of Aguzzi. He came up in the business in Sicily as a made man. Ruthless, No conscience. No mercy. Police, Carabinieri, FBI- nobody could catch him, or stop him. If you thought Winter was bad, this guy makes him look like a fluffy soft kitten."

My guts tightened, my stomach rolling in sickness. Jolene froze. High ranking mobsters shifted uneasily in their seats.

Billy added, "He's a killing machine. Anyone in his way."

"So, what does this monster look like?", a voice quizzed. "If you don't have a picture of him, how the hell are we supposed to recognize him if walks into our casino, Mr. Gorman?" There seemed to be a collective grumble, agreement around the table.

The boss paced the room. "I have been told a little bit about him. Orphan, no known family. Like me. Raised on the streets since he was 10. Came up fast because he would take the jobs other found too messy. His MO is: he loves knives. The thrill of blood pouring out a severed part gives him satisfaction. He has dark hair, naturally curly. Slightly on the heavy side. Likes good food. A large scar down his cheek from a knife fight to assume the Don position. Obviously, he won. Carabinieri and Interpol have been pouring the heat on him. We don't know what Winter promised him for his services, but rumor has it he will be awarded a whole new life – including facial reconstruction and protection."

A gruff snarl from a man I didn't recognize spoke, "And the two broads? Did that issue get resolved?" The disdain was not hidden in any way. Jolene squirmed.

"No," Darius replied firmly.

The man who obviously did not like Jolene and myself barked, "I knew those two were trouble from the very beginning."

Billy reaffirmed, "I chose this trouble, not them. Don't forget that."

It was awkward, tense, and I just wanted to discreetly slip away. Darius grinned. Who would dare to challenge Billy Gorman or his position as mob boss of Las Vegas? The room quickly fell into compliance.

"I know this isn't much to go on," Darius said, taking over. "But we felt it was important enough for each of you to be fully aware of this issue. You can go but know that more information is coming, and we will fill you in as soon as it is available."

The head of security for the casino stood up first and turned his body directly to me and Jolene. I waited for yet another nasty comment in angst. He dipped his head to one side slowly. "Congratulations on making it to the table. You're in the game up to your necks now. Be ready."

His words took me back and I could not come up with a response to his acknowledgment. The room emptied of all players except Billy, Darius, Jolene, Roderick and me.

There was a silent exchange between the men that I did not understand. Roderick announced, "If that will be all sir, I shall see you at the house. I will pour you a whiskey and have it waiting." He exited, leaving us.

In a haunting tone, I questioned, "Is there anything we can do, Billy?"

Barrington said flatly, "Pray." He took Jolene's hand gently. "Let's go home."

CHAPTER 2

Things had gone quiet in the mob war. Trent Winter didn't make any more aggressive moves toward our organization. It surprised me because everybody was talking about Aguzzi. Horror stories of his life in Sicily came to light, his ruthless demeanor became well known. But still no one knew his face.

My nightmares settled down in the silence, although occasionally I would dream of Ken Parks torturing me and waking up screaming and gasping for air. Billy was gentle when this happened, holding me tenderly in his arms until the terror faded away in the night.

Darius reminded us not to ever let our guard down- for Trent Winter was a patient man and willing to wait it out until an opportune moment struck.

Billy and Darius had grown weary of our 2 disks and trying to access the information on them. They spent less time locked in the office and on the computer. Sometimes I asked the boss if I could help him decipher the information. He flatly declined my offer. I found this really annoying. After all, the disks did belong to me and perhaps I could help figure out what my father's codes were. Now, the disks spent more time in the safe than the computer.

Life was good. Maybe we finally earned a shot at normalcy.

Stepping from my morning shower, I gazed at my reflection in the mirror. I was lost in thought, staring at every scar Ken Parks had left on me. Some were deep and ugly like the ones on my back from the lashes of the bullwhip he beat me with. Others were subtle like the small cigarette burns on my skin. A sigh escaped my lips. Memories flooded back. Torcher. Rape. But the worst scars were the ones you could not see. The psychological effects would live in me forever and would never fade away totally.

Billy touched my shoulder gently and I jumped, pulling back wildly with shock. I had forgotten he was still in the room. Softly he asked, "Why do you do this to yourself, Jasmine?"

"Do what?", I quizzed in a whisper, knowing full well what he meant.

"You stand in this mirror every morning baby and stare at those scars. It's like you're re-living it every day. What happened to you and Jolene was terrible. Let me find a good plastic surgeon. We can get rid of a lot of these scars."

"I know you think I'm ugly now."

"Jasmine, I love you. I don't care if you have marks on you. I want to help you get over this and heal. Let's get a doctor to see what we can do."

"No," I answered in a hollow and haunted tone. "No. I need to keep these."

"Why?" His voice turned to frustration. "Why the hell wouldn't you want to get rid of those lash marks on your back. It makes no fucking sense."

Refusing to get into a big debate, I turned away from him and glared into the mirror once more.

"Jasmine!" Gorman demanded.

I whispered, "I need these, Billy. I need these to remind me every day that my life is never going to be safe again. It reminds me I have to be stronger, smarter, and more determined than the enemy."

"That's not healthy, babe." Gorman snared his shirt and walked away, while I gazed at my reflection in silence.

I got dressed and followed the boss down to the kitchen. Roderick already had coffee on the table. Rosita bustled in. "Good morning, what can I get everyone for breakfast? I have some fresh baked muffins and fruit."

Darius had his face buried in the morning paper. Jolene kicked my leg under the table, eyes glazed over and wide. She must have some kind of hang over, I thought.

Rosita continued, "Miss Jasmine, Miss Jolene would you care for something? Pancakes? Eggs? I can make an omelet or French toast." Rosita was a wonderful cook and a fine maid. She was trying so hard, but nobody seemed to be listening.

Barrington responded, "No time this morning, Rosie, Gorman and I have a meeting in an hour at the casino with the gaming commission."

"Did we have a violation again?", Gorman sighed.

"When don't we? No, just our monthly warning to go straight or else. We have their pay off."

Billy nodded, uninterested.

Jolene kicked me again under the table. Her eyes were pleading with me, but no words.

"Stop it," I barked at my sister.

The newspaper lowered and Barrington peered at us over the top of it. He then glanced to Jolene. She sputtered, "Somebody's cranky this morning."

"We have to go, or we'll be late. We also have a staff meeting."

The guys gathered their things and left without another word. Rosita disappeared, grumbling about nobody loved her cooking anymore. Roderick announced, "I will be in the office. I have to do financials today."

Soon the room emptied, and it was just us at the kitchen table. "What the hell is wrong with you?", I snapped.

She gritted her teeth. Jolene snarled in a hushed voice, "We gotta talk."

"So, talk", I muttered, slurping down coffee.

"Not here. Some place private." It was at this moment I realized that what she had to say was very important and very confidential. The seriousness of her tone grabbed my attention real fast.

"Follow me." She led me thorough the house quickly, dragging me by the hand. She found the one spot we had discovered was not covered by the security cameras, near the garden.

"Ok," I blurted out, tired of the secrecy. "What is it? What is so damn important that you're frigging kicking me under the table like a mad woman? Huh? What the hell is going on?"

For a minute, Jolene was unable to speak, biting her lip nervously. I raised my hands in anger and turned to walk away. She snared my arm, pulling me in close to her. "Remember when we went to Hawaii?", she asked, looking over her shoulder to make sure there was no one around. I nodded, shooting her a pissed off side-eye. She shifted uncomfortably. "I forgot to pack my birth control pills and didn't have the nerve to tell Darius." I instantly stiffened, now at full attention. "I missed my period."

My head dropped, my chin hitting my chest. "By how much? Maybe it's just stress, you know?"

"By 9 weeks."

"Jolene, that's not 1 period, that's 2!"

"I know," she sputtered, tears in her eyes. "What am I going to do? Billy will be furious at me. You know how he preached to us about being consistent. Darius is gonna be mad as hell at me because I didn't tell him I forgot my pills. I just kept telling him I wasn't ready after Trent Winter raped me, but there were a few times that I just wanted to be with Darius. I just threw caution to the wind. I told myself that it was so few times that I couldn't possibly get pregnant on 3 or 4 times of making love. I'm in trouble, Jasmine. Big trouble. You have to help me!" She was in a panicked frenzy, begging and pleading. Tears ran down her face.

I put my hand on my forehead in disbelief. Our eyes locked and I ran my fingers through my hair, pulling back my bangs and exhaling loudly. "Oh shit, Jolene," I blurted out.

"What am I going to do?", she cried.

I started biting my nails, shifting my feet. "Well," I muttered, "First off, we don't even know for sure if you are pregnant. Maybe it just got messed up because of Winter."

"Jasmine," her voice trembled. "I don't know how to tell Darius. I know he will be so mad."

"We need to get a pregnancy test," I concluded.

"We can't let anyone know," my sister flushed. "Not until I know for sure."

"We'll ask Roderick to take us to the pharmacy."

"No!' We can't! He'll tell Billy and Darius for sure. No. No. That can't happen. We have to find another way." This was a real problem. "Look, Roderick is doing the monthly financial stuff. That always takes him about an hour. The pharmacy is only about 15 minutes away. We can take Dad's corvette. We can shoot over there really quick. In and out; back in 35 minutes. Nobody will ever know."

"And what do we tell the front gate guards? We're just going for a country drive?? Hhmmmm?"

Silence fell upon us both. We tapped our feet, the wheels in our brains turning.

"Well," she offered, "we can tell the guards that the Vette needed to be taken for a short 5-minute spin, just to turn over the tires and distribute the oil because it has sat too long."

"And when they ask who gave us permission to leave by ourselves to do that?"

"We're only going to be gone a few minutes. We'll tell them Roderick said it was ok. Boom, boom. We go, we get the test, and we're back in no time. Problem solved. I have to know for sure. If I'm not pregnant, then we never have to mention this to Darius or Billy. Nobody will ever know but you and me, sis."

"I don't know. I'm not sure I like this idea, Jolene. If the guys find out, I'm pretty sure they'll be pissed."

"And if I get them all riled up and I don't even know for sure if I am or not?? You know the shit is going to hit the fan." I groaned. "Please," she begged me. I closed my eyelids and nodded. "We'll only be in the store one second."

"I'll get the keys," I surrendered.

I sat behind the steering wheel of the corvette. I hadn't driven Dad's car in so long. The wheel felt good in my hands. The engine purred, coming to life. As I backed out of the garage, the feeling of freedom rushed through my veins. Gorman, Barrington, and Roderick had kept us on such a short leash. We rolled the windows down and let the breeze fly through our hair, turning up the radio.

Pulling up to the front gate, the guards grilled us with their eyes. "Where are you going?" he interrogated. Jolene's story just fell out of her mouth so fluid and unrehearsed, assuring him that we were only going a few feet beyond the gate and turning right around to come back. He questioned us suspiciously, asking who gave authorization.

"Oh, Roderick knows," Jolene reassured, in the biggest lie ever.

The guard grunted with mild disbelief. "If you say so." He raised the gate and we drove through with no other restraints.

"Slow down," Jolene yelled at me as we whizzed down the road. "We don't need a speeding ticket. Do you want to explain a ticket to Billy?"

I immediately reduced my speed as we made our way to the pharmacy. The feeling was so uplifting to not be attached to the guys. My heart was jumping with joy. I parked in the space close to the pharmacy door and we both sprinted inside. Jolene quickly got the pregnancy test kit and had it in hand when we turned down the make up isle. She giggled, "Look at this awful color, Jas. Can't you see me wearing this? Look, I'm a circus clown."

I laughed, picking up a set of huge false eyelashes. "What do you think?", I asked, chuckling. She snickered, as we took multiple items off of the shelf and put them back. Suddenly, I remembered our timeline. How long had we been goofing off and looking at makeup? Roderick was usually done in an hour. "Hey, we gotta go. Right now!" We went to the register, but now the line was backed up and there was a lady arguing with the cashier about a refund. Finally, Jolene paid for the pregnancy test kit, and we headed for the corvette.

At the casino, the meetings had all ended for Gorman and Barrington. They sat alone in the conference room. Billy turned to his friend. "Darius, I'm worried about Jasmine. I offered to get plastic surgery for the wounds Parks left behind. She refused. She said they remind her to be strong and smart."

Barrington tipped his head to one side. "You want me to talk to her, boss?"

Gorman shrugged. "I don't know. It's like those bastards are still in her head. Maybe she needs a shrink to talk to."

Darius said, "I don't know, Billy. Is there anyone we can trust with this? This isn't just some absent father figure complex. Those girls went through hell. And what about the disks? We can't have word of that getting out. Other organizations might not understand why we didn't share this with them."

"I can't stand to see her this way, Darius."

"You must remember, Billy, those assholes damaged the girls. It's up to us to fix that damage. So maybe it's true?"

"What's true?"

"Maybe Billy Gorman really is in love?"

"Well, I'm definitely in lust," he grinned as they exited the conference room.

Time was getting really short for us and now I was getting nervous that Roderick might finish early. We jogged to the car. The parking lot had filled now, and our vehicle was sandwiched in between two big black vans. I yanked the keys from my pocket of my blue jeans. We were laughing and talking about the shopping experience. I pushed the door lock button on the key fob and reminded Jolene that we had spent too much time inside the store. It was time to get back home.

As we got to the car, the van's sliding doors opened on both sides of us. Two men with their faces covered in masks and holding guns jumped out at me on the driver's side. On the passenger's side, Jolene was grabbed by two assailants, and they were stuffing her into the van. She screamed and fought back, their hands covering her face. Panicking, I tried to run around the back of the corvette to get to her and free her.

Jolene's attackers were pulling her into the van. I called out her name, horrified, at the top of my lungs.

One of the men produced a huge bowie knife, holding it to her throat menacingly. Jolene ceased thrashing about and collapsed, compliant. I had visions of Ken Parks slicing my dad's throat in front of me. He had dark, curly hair and an evil smile I could see below the mask. He tore the mask off and tossed it to the ground confidently. As he turned to face me, I could see the long scar running down his face. Spital flying from his sneering lips, he warned. "I'll gut her like a fish." I froze, my heart pounding and tears welling up in my eyes.

Suddenly the sound of gunshots pierced the air. As if in slow motion, bullet holes pinged the van. So many bullets, I lost count. Several of the bullets found their mark, and all of the kidnappers went down except for Aguzzi. Blood splattered all over Aguzzi and the van from his fallen associates. In the distraction, the knife fell from his hand as he withdrew his own handgun to return fire. He still had Jolene by the torso, and she bit his forearm with all she had, spitting out a chunk of flesh. With the sudden rush of pain in his arm, he let go of her.

A black Cadillac Escalade squealed to a halt behind us. "Get in!", a voice shouted at us. "Get in!", it repeated sternly. I glanced over my shoulder. I knew that voice and I had never been so happy to see his face.

Roderick swung the door open for us. We jumped into the moving vehicle, and he drove away wildly, side swiping two parked cars. The sound of gunshot rang out behind us as Sal Aguzzi was shooting at us in our escape. The back windshield shattered. The Cadillac jumped the curb and tour up a median, blasting through a red light, narrowly missing oncoming traffic.

"Fuck," Roderick exclaimed. We were being pursued by the van. "Get down," he ordered, driving erratically in and out of traffic. In seconds, a police car pulled up in pursuit of our parade. The police were right on the van's bumper. Roderick turned down a narrow alleyway, just missing on coming cars. The van plowed over three pedestrians. Bodies flew in the air. He popped out of the alley and made a hard left-hand turn. The van and the police were still right behind us. From a side street, a box truck was pulling out and we barely made it around it. The van wasn't so lucky and collided with the truck and crashed; the police vehicle smashing into the back of the van. I looked back through the shattered back windshield and saw several police cars surrounding the van. The strip was coming into sight. Roderick made several quick turns and was soon zooming down the freeway.

"Are you alright?", Roderick shouted. Stunned, we sat dazed and silent. "Are you alright?", he repeated; more concerned.

"Yeah, I think so", I answered.

"Fuck!", Roderick sneered. He never swore around us before. His face was red and twisted with rage and concern. Jolene and I glanced at each other in fear. We were in big trouble now.

CHAPTER 3

Roderick was super angry, driving fast down the highway to an unknown destination. A knot formed in the pit of my gut when I realized we were driving away from the city and not towards the Gorman estate.

30 minutes later the shot-up Cadillac came to rest in a wooded remote area near Lake Mead. We were in silence the entire drive and terrified as to what was to come.

"Get out!", he shouted, still seething in rage. Slowly we opened the bullet ridden door and sheepishly stood next to the vehicle. He pointed to a nearby picnic table at the water's edge. "Get your asses over there now", he demanded.

Cautiously, we made our way to the picnic table. My mind was spinning. I was almost positive he was going to put a bullet in our head and dump our bodies in the lake.

"Sit down!" Jolene and I slid onto the top of table, placing our feet on the seats.

"I can explain," my sister offered.

Roderick's face was dripping sweat, red, and the veins in his neck were protruding. I had never seen him enraged like this and frankly, it scared me. My heart was racing.

Ignoring Jolene's offer of explanation, he yelled at us like a dragon breathing a fiery revenge out of his mouth. "What the hell are you trying to do? Are you fucking trying to get me killed?", he blasted.

I blinked in silence at his wrath. "What happened to your accent?", Jolene questioned.

He took two steps towards the table, and I thought this was the end. Even Ken Parks never intimidated me like this. Roderick was like a possessed demon.

"Haven't you figured it out yet?", he screamed. We cowered before him, whimpering softly. "Don't you know it's my job to protect you two? I'm not some stupid butler, damn it! I am third in command of Gorman's organization! I accepted this bullshit request of Gorman because he needed someone, he could trust to watch over you, to keep you safe when he had to be gone. My sole fucking purpose in life is to protect you two and you do <u>this</u> to me?!"

He paced back and forth nervously, letting this new revelation sink in. "Gorman is going to kill me for this." He glared at us with cold fury. "Don't you realize what you've done?", he exploded.

Jolene blubbered and wailed in tears saying she was sorry over and over again. Suddenly, everything made sense. That's why he was at the Sal Aguzzi briefing. I felt sick. I wanted to throw up. "We didn't know," I said quietly.

"What on earth is so damn important that you two idiots would pull this stunt? Do I now have to keep you locked up in that shark cage all day, every day because I can no longer trust you? I thought we had a great trust built up between us, ladies. Why?"

His shoulders slumped, his knees went weak, and he nearly hit the ground. "You're not a butler," I sighed, rubbing my eyes.

"My name is Kevin Williams. I am under Barrington, and I run a lot of our less than legal operations from behind the scenes. I am a made man turned into a fucking babysitter for you two ungrateful little bitches. I don't know why I don't shoot you right now!"

Again, he began pacing and mumbling to himself that Billy was going to kill him. He came to a quick halt, only a foot away from us. "Why?", he snarled. "Why?"

Tears streamed down Jolene's face. Barely audible, she whined, "I needed a pregnancy test. I think I'm pregnant."

Roderick gawked at us, a maniacal chuckle coming from his throat. "Are you fucking serious?", he spat, "why didn't you just fucking tell me?!"

"I didn't want the guys to get upset until I knew for sure. You know how Billy is, Roderick …er, Kevin. I didn't want to rile them up if I'm not pregnant. Nobody would ever know, and everything would be ok."

"Oh yeah?", he snarled, "How'd that work out for you?" He placed his hands on his hips, breathing into her face, inches away.

"We couldn't tell you. You would have told Darius and Billy!", she cried. "I'm sorry."

"You're sorry and I'm dead. I can't believe this happened on my watch." He started pacing again. "I am responsible for you guys; don't you understand that? You almost got taken or killed, and it would have been <u>my</u> fault."

In this instant we realized we had made a huge mistake. Jolene cried uncontrollably. Roderick locked eyes with me, still so pissed off. Flatly, he interrogated, "Did you get the damn test?" I nodded yes, still too terrified to speak. Barely above a whisper, Kevin sighed, "You have no idea how bad this is going to be. Get back in the car. We're all going to have to answer for this."

It was dead calm in the vehicle all the way back to the Gorman estate, only the sound of the road whine under our tires. My brain had a hard time wrapping itself around Kevin's confession. I processed all that he told me and was angry with myself for not recognizing the signs that had been before us in plain sight all along. Wave after wave of guilt flooded over me. Roderick had always been so nice to us. Why hadn't I seen the signs before? His whole purpose was to protect us, and we had violated that sacred trust. My head hurt and my stomach turned in nausea.

Pulling into the Gorman estate, the gate guards shot us an evil glance and gaped at the bullet holes in the Escalade. I knew they were going to be in trouble too for not stopping us when we left the grounds unaccompanied.

We came to rest in the driveway. Roderick made a call on his cellphone. "I need someone to come get the keys to the Corvette and retrieve the car from the pharmacy parking lot." My eyes had been opened and now I saw everything crystal clear.

We hadn't been back but a few minutes when Billy and Darius pulled up. Gorman slowly got out, walking past the Cadillac and staring at the bullet holes. Barrington was right on his heels. "I just got a call from the mayor," Gorman growled, "It seems my vehicle was involved in a moving shoot out with 2 dead and several people injured. He's now up my ass, threatening to shut my casino down and prosecute my entire organization. Anybody want to tell me what the hell happened here today?"

I noticed that we had several staff members gathered around us now to view the fiasco.

Barrington turned to the growing crowd of observers. "Go back to work. Nothing to see here," he ordered sharply. They scattered like a flock of birds at his command. "Let's take this inside," he instructed.

Rosita was in the kitchen as our rag tag group entered. "Good afternoon, Mr. Gorman. You're home early," she smiled. "May I get you a glass of lemonade?"

"Get out!" he snapped harshly.

Barrington gave a cold look to his boss. Rosita had tears in her eyes, wiping her hands on her apron and scampered off, heartbroken at his cruel tone. Darius gave Jolene and me the hand signal to sit down at the table and we quickly did so. Roderick (Kevin) stood behind us, facing Billy and Darius.

Barrington said, "Ok. Everybody just calm down and go over this step by step. What happened?" Nobody wanted to speak. The long silence was deafening. Gorman was building up pressure and about to explode.

Roderick (Kevin) answered calmly. "There was an incident today, Billy." Roderick placed his hand on each of our shoulders. "You see we went to the store to get a few supplies and there was a surprise attack. I'm pretty sure it was Salvatore."

"Did you see Winter?"

"No. Actually, it looked like Salvatore was running the operation. Winter was nowhere to be found." There was a dreadful pause. "They tried to get the girls but failed. Yes, we had some gunfire and a bit of a chase, but everything turned out ok."

"Ok? Ok?", Gorman flooded. "My car is filled with bullet holes and the mayor is on my ass again! That's not ok!"

"Let's stay calm, Billy," Barrington directed. Gorman put his hands on his hips.

"That's it? That's what you have for me?", the boss questioned in rage. Roderick replied softly, "That's it."

Billy stomped across the floor at him with anger and purpose. He got right in Roderick's face and growled, "If this ever happens again, you know the consequences."

"Yes sir," he whispered, gulping.

"You are dismissed," he snapped. Kevin nodded silently and slipped from the room. He hadn't told Billy about our deception, about the pregnancy test, or about our livid conversation at Lake Mead. He hadn't told the boss any of it.

Billy and Darius sat at the table across from Jolene and me. The boss pulled out his 45 and sat it in the center of the table gently. "Who's going to tell me what really happened here today?", Gorman asked softly.

His eyes burned straight through me. I flinched, sputtering, "Roderick told you what happened."

"Bullshit! If I don't get the truth in one minute, you're not going to like what I do next."

Barrington announced, "40 seconds, 30…." He was looking at his watch in a maddening countdown. "20…"

Like dam waters cresting a floodgate, Jolene spat out flabbergasted, "It's all my fault! I did it! I thought I might be pregnant, so we slipped out when Kevin was in the office. I just wanted to get a pregnancy test, that's all. We thought we would go and be right back, but they were waiting for us outside the store. Then Kevin pulled up and started shooting and saved us, and then we went to the Lake and now we're here." She was exasperated and breathless, talking fast. It came flying out of her like a volcano erupting its lava. She was sobbing and gasping. "Please don't be mad at Kevin, it's all my fault."

Darius narrowed his eyes at her. "You keep calling him Kevin. So now you know. He was not supposed to tell you."

"Please," she begged him, "please don't kill him. It's my fault. Kill me." Another long silence fell across the room. A lump formed in my throat.

"All of this because you thought you might be pregnant?" Darius broke out into laughter, repeating, "Pregnant."

Gorman turned to his number one and sneered, "You think this is funny?! Take care of it, Barrington!" Darius nodded, standing and pulling Jolene to her feet, escorting her out of the room. I could tell the boss was fuming and I shifted uncomfortably under his gaze.

Billy addressed me, "It's good you know about Kevin, but if you ever pull this shit again, I am going to put a bullet between his eyes." He stood and started to walk away, then turned back to me, glaring. "You the one who came up with this hair brain idea?" I shook my head no, throwing my sister under the bus. "I'm surprised," he added coldly. "And the truth shall set you free." He walked away without another word. I broke down in tears. With the room empty, I no longer needed to be the strong one and I bawled like a baby.

It was a sleepless night. I tossed and turned. Every time sleep would close in on me, I could see Salvatore's face. I wondered and pondered many things- living the day's events over and over in my mind. Why wasn't Trent Winter there? How did they know Jolene and I would be at the pharmacy alone? The whole mess was unsettling.

Morning breakfast could not have been any more quiet and awkward. It was horrible. Billy and Darius were silent, obviously still very angry. Roderick stood close by, not saying a word, ready to take whatever punishment they decided to hand out. Rosita sniffled back tears, too terrified to give a greeting or offer food. Jolene hung her head in shame, as I stared blankly at the wall, not making eye contact with anybody.

Minutes seemed like hours. "So," Gorman finally broke the ice, "Is she pregnant?" All eyes in the room turned to my sister, cutting her down to size.

"Yes," Barrington sighed. "We'll take care of it."

From out of the blue, I spoke up, "How did they know we were at the pharmacy alone? Jolene and I didn't even know until we were in the car. How could they possibly know what we were doing? Tracking device?"

"Not likely, or they would've already had you," Darius replied.

"But then how?", I quizzed. "We didn't tell anyone, not even Roderick."

"The front gate knew," Roderick announced. "The fucking front gate knew. We have a spy, who's reporting our coming and going to Trent Winter."

Billy's eyes narrowed on Kevin. "You know what to do." I was terrified to ask any more questions.

CHAPTER 4

As Gorman stood to leave, his cellphone went off. Groaning over caller ID, he answered, "Good morning, mayor. Yes, I know what happened yesterday. It was an attempted robbery. The girls were out shopping, when thugs tried to mug them. It was just by luck that Roderick happened by and saw what was going down. Simple case of self-defense. I don't know what possessed the muggers to plow into the group of pedestrians. That was very unfortunate. They must've been on drugs is all I can figure. And the suspect, do you still have him in custody? Bailed out already, huh? Yes, the girls are fine, mayor. Thank you very much for your concern. Of course, you can count on us for a healthy donation to the police benevolent society. Yes. Thank you again, mayor." Gorman hung up the phone, grumbling, "And they say we shouldn't shake people down." The boss grabbed his briefcase, heading towards the door. "Take care of business here, Barrington, and I'll see you at the casino later." Darius nodded in silence, lost in his coffee cup.

Roderick came into the kitchen, fixing a cup of coffee for himself.

Jolene whispered, "Why didn't you even ask him Darius?"

"You heard him, Jolene," Barrington sighed.

"I don't want to give this baby up."

"I don't either, Jolene, but sometimes we have no choices."

"I hate him," she sniffled, tears welling up in her eyes.

"Jolene!", Barrington scolded. She jumped to her feet and ran out the door.

"Is this under control?", Roderick asked, concerned there was going to be trouble.

"No, not at all," Darius replied in a hollow tone. "She told me that she wants to die now, so I'm on suicide watch. And you know what? Right now, I hate Gorman too."

Darius sat his cup down on the table and took off after Jolene.

Roderick sighed, "Oh boy, my job just keeps getting tougher and tougher. You two girls are going to be the death of me yet."

A few minutes later, Barrington poked his head inside the kitchen. "Roderick, I've got Jolene. We're going now. We'll be back later." Roderick tipped his head in acknowledgment.

I spun around in my seat and gazed at him standing behind me. Our eyes locked. "Whatever it is you're thinking, Jasmine, the answer is no."

"You heard them. If they go through with this, they will both hate Billy forever. Nothing will ever be the same and it will destroy us. I'm going to ask Gorman to reconsider and let them keep this child."

He slowly placed his coffee on the counter. "That's not a good idea, Jasmine. This is their battle and their decision. You should not get involved."

"You heard them. They think they don't have a choice."

"No."

"I have to try. I'm leaving with or without your permission Kevin." He folded his arms across his chest at the challenge, glaring at me. "Please," I pleaded, hoping to avoid a huge fight. "I have to try before it's too late. If he still says no, I will comply." I stood up and we squared off face to face.

"Are you seriously challenging me Jasmine, after yesterday? You do not want to piss me off. I'm still upset with you two after yesterday's shenanigans."

I squared my shoulders in defiance, not backing down. "I don't want to fight you, Jasmine, but I will if I need to." Tense moments passed as he pondered the situation. "Are we really going to do this?"

25

"All I want is a chance to ask him, Kevin. That's all. Just give me the chance." My shoulders slumped in submission.

He shifted his feet, sighing, "Get your coat." He rolled his eyes, mumbling, "You're really pushing your luck around here."

The casino was jumping with business, even though it was early in the day. We made our way towards Billy's private office. A guard told us he was in the conference room. Through the glass doors, I could see him talking to a small group of people. He caught a glimpse of me and Roderick waiting outside. "You still have time to change your mind, Jasmine", Roderick whispered. "He seems in a nasty mood already. You're the one living with the consequences." He wasn't going to take responsibility for the interruption.

I hesitated at the door. My hands were trembling, my stomach churning, dropping acid by the gallons. Maybe I should follow Roderick's advice. No, I had to do this. I had to try for everyone's sake. I knocked on the conference room door and stepped inside. All talking ceased.

With a low voice, I announced, "I'm sorry to disturb you, but can I please speak with you for a moment, Mr. Gorman?"

"Jasmine, I'm in a meeting, can't this wait?" A glance of annoyance was directed at me.

"I really need to talk to you now, please." The boss passed a sharp look to Roderick, who merely shrugged his shoulders.

Gorman tossed his hands in the air. "Meeting adjourned. We will reconvene tomorrow." The room emptied. Frustrated, he sighed, "What do you want, Jasmine?"

"I've come to ask you to please reconsider letting Jolene and Darius keep the baby."

"What?"

I took a deep breath as Roderick sat in a chair staring out of the window. I was on my own. "They both want to keep the baby, and if you tell them they can't, you are going to ruin everything that we have here, Billy."

He tipped his head to one side, placing his hand on his hip. "And what exactly is it that we have here, Jasmine?"

Softly, I replied, "Family. We're family, Billy."

Roderick muttered, "Yup, real nice weather we're having here." He wasn't going to touch this conversation. Gorman smirked at me, mocking me.

"You have to stop them before it's too late. They are already on their way. Hurry."

"Did I ever say they could not keep the baby?", he asked.

"Don't you play coy with me, Billy Gorman," I snapped. "You said take care of it, and everybody knew what that meant!"

"Well, aren't you feisty today," the boss grinned. He leaned in close to me and said, "Don't forget who you're talking to, Jasmine." His threat cut right through me, and I went weak in the knees.

I softened and added in a hollow tone, "I thought we were the good guys, Billy. If you make them kill their child, I will never be able to look in your eyes and not see Ken Parks staring back at me."

I took a step towards the door, and he snared my bicep. Ouch. That cut him down to size. Tenderly he whispered, "I see why you drove Parks crazy. If I do this, will you stop being a pain in my ass?" He pulled out his cellphone and dialed Barrington. After a few rings the boss spoke, "He has it turned off."

I implored him, "We can drive over there in person."

"You really do know how to push my buttons."

"Ain't that the truth," Roderick muttered.

"All right, damn it," he sighed.

The car hadn't even come to a rest, when I threw open the door and leapt out. I burst through the front door of the clinic and rushed to the front desk. "Jolene Grant and Darius Barrington where are they?", I gasped, out of breath.

The nurse blinked at me, and responded dryly, "They are in the procedure room. You will have to wait for them to come out." I glance over my shoulder, observing the sign pointing to the procedure area. Sprinting down the hallway towards the procedure rooms, I could hear the nurse calling out to me. "Wait! Stop! You can't go back there!"

As the nurse rounded the desk to pursue me, Gorman blocked her path and pulled back his jacket to reveal his gun. "I say she can," he spat. The nurse came to a quick halt, recognizing Gorman. "We're just here to talk. Go back to work." The nurse glanced down the hall, not wanting to ignore her duties. "I said go back to your desk."

She groaned and followed his instructions.

I pushed open the door calling out to Jolene and Darius loudly, bellowing their names out for all to hear. Barrington stepped from the room. "Jasmine, what the hell are you doing here?"

"Stop! You don't have to do this! Billy said you can keep the baby. It' ok."

"What?", Barrington questioned, confused. "Are you sure?"

"I'm sure," Gorman answered, entering the hallway behind me.

A huge smile curled up on Barrington's lips, shouting, "Jolene, stop!" He bounded back into the procedure room and was gone for just a moment, then returning gave us a big thumbs up. "We made it in time," he laughed. Darius's face lit up like a Christmas tree, joy oozing out of him.

Billy took my arm and led me back to the nurse's station. She stood up to confront us but kept her silence. Gorman nodded to her as we exited the building. Outside, Gorman whispered to me, "You girls are going to be the death of me yet." Why did everyone keep saying that?

I gave him a big hug. "I can't thank you enough, Billy."

"Oh, you will," he smirked. "Let me tell you, Jasmine: if you ever wondered about my love for you- today was your proof." I kissed his lips. "Now get outta here and let me go back to work."

NEW YORK CITY: Trent Winter was seated in the private back room to a smokey bar. Stacks of cash covered the table before him. He was surrounded by several of his top men. There was a knock on the door and Salvatore stepped inside, sheepishly.

"You wanted to see me?"

"Everybody out and close the door behind you." He motioned Sal to sit down. Tension was in the air. Winter leaned back in his chair. He carefully placed his fingertips together, glaring at Aguzzi. "Tell me why we're having this conversation."

Aguzzi held his hands up in defense of Winter's harsh tone. "I know you said to wait for your go ahead on the Gorman girls, boss," he explained, "but an opportunity arose that should've been perfect. The gate guard said they were alone. When will we ever get a chance like that, Trent?"

"So why don't you have them?"

"Well, all of a sudden, this SUV pulls up and starts shooting at us. Killed Tony. Jolene, that little bitch bit a chunk out of my arm." He held up his bandaged arm to offer proof. "All my guys are returning fire, and someone starts yelling from inside the vehicle for the girls to get in. Somehow, they managed to slip away from us in the chaos. We chased them through the streets, but the cops showed up. The weird thing is: the driver looked like the damn butler."

"Butler? The butler beat 4 of my men in a running shootout. Interesting. Get me everything you have on this butler."

"Yes, boss." He stood to leave.

Winter stopped him. "You do nothing, and I mean <u>nothing</u> without my order – do you understand me? You screwed the pooch on this, Sal. This complicates my plans, because now they've seen your face."

"I'm sorry, Mr. Winter. It's like some miracle they got away."

Trent Winter gave a knowing sneer. "Been there, done that. That's why I told you we need finesse."

Aguzzi shuffled out, afraid to turn his back to Winter. He closed the door and left Trent in silence. Trent took a picture of the girls out of his pocket and stared at their faces, sipping from a glass of whiskey. "Why are you my biggest challenge?", he mused to himself. "Always elusive, just at my fingertips, but always out of reach, torturing me." A big smile took over his face as he touched the photo and slid it back into his pocket.

CHAPTER 5

Jolene and Darius were abuzz with excitement and joy at the new life forming in her. They giggled and made eyes at each other, kissing and hugging like teenage sweethearts.

Gorman stared at them intently over his coffee. He had never seen Barrington happier and more alive. Roderick chuckled over their antics, as Gorman just seemed annoyed. "All right, love birds, we have work to do," Billy announced, standing to leave. The boss turned to Roderick and said, "Call me on my cell in an hour."

"Yes, sir," Roderick acknowledged – showing serious concern.

When Billy and Darius were gone, I asked Roderick, "So am I in trouble again?" He shrugged his shoulders evasively and walked out of the room.

Jolene bubbled over all day, talking about baby names and cute baby clothes. I laughed at her eagerness, pointing out she still had months to go.

As soon as the guys returned, Gorman announced, "Roderick, Darius – meeting in the office now. Jasmine and Jolene, we won't be long. Sit tight for a few minutes." There was a seriousness in his tone.

When they vanished into the office, Jolene gulped, "Damn, I hope Billy didn't change his mind about letting us keep the baby."

The three men entered the office, closing the door behind them. "Have a seat, Darius," the boss instructed. Gorman sat atop his desk, facing him, while Roderick hovered off to the side.

Barrington gazed at the two men staring him down. "So, ok, what's going on?", he questioned cautiously.

"Kevin and I have been talking about this baby."

Darius's shoulders slumped, assuming they had changed their mind. Billy continued, "We both feel that it is going to change the entire dynamic of how we do things in this house." Barrington's face held his disappointment.

Kevin quickly responded, "Darius, we're not saying you can't keep this baby. We just want you to be fully aware of how this will change things."

"I know there will be challenges," he defended. "But I really don't want to give this child up."

Gorman spoke up, "Roderick and I have been observing you, Darius. We've never seen you so happy before. So, we need to ask you if you love this woman."

"Of course, I do," Barrington sputtered, offended.

"Then since you obviously feel that way, we believe you need to follow this thing through." Relief poured over him, but Darius was confused, sure there was more to this conversation.

Roderick stated, "You know I am responsible for those girls, and frankly, I have become quite fond of them, despite that little ruse they pulled the other day. So, Gorman and I had a little talk today when you were on the casino floor."

Barrington raised one eyebrow. "What's going on here? What are you saying?"

Billy responded, "We want to know if you plan on marrying Jolene."

Barrington laughed, "That's what this is all about? You want to know if my intentions are honorable? A little late for that, now, isn't it?"

Gorman's face held no humor. "Put a ring on it, Darius." This wasn't a joke to Gorman.

Darius said, "Yes, I love her, and if you two give your permission, then yes. I will marry her."

"Sooner, rather than later," Kevin added.

"That's all," the boss concluded. "Send Rosita in please. I've got some damage control to do with her." Barrington nodded and left the room, closing the door behind him. As he got to the other side, a huge grin broke out on his face. They were defending Jolene's honor. He thought that was a cute gesture on their part.

Rosita entered the office, wringing her hands nervously. "You wanted to see me, Mr. Gorman?"

"Relax. You're not in trouble Rosie. I actually called you in because I want to ask a favor of you."

"Of course, Mr. Gorman, how can I help you?"

"I'm sure you have heard by now that Jolene is pregnant."

"Yes," she flooded, "very exciting. I am so happy."

"I know your position here is technically our cook and maid. However, I wonder if you would be willing to help Jolene and Jasmin out with the baby when it comes."

"Oh," she squealed, "I would love to!"

"There will obviously be compensation."

Roderick explained, "The girls don't have a mother to give them advice and I know that you have 3 children of your own. They may need someone to help guide them on what to do occasionally. Maybe even to babysit when called upon."

"Those girls are like my own. I would be thrilled to do it."

"Thank you," Billy winked at her, "That will be all for now, Rosie." She sashayed from the office filled with pride that they would entrust her with such a task.

Everyone had walked out of the meetings with a smile on their faces. As Roderick and Billy entered the kitchen, I quizzed, "Are all the meetings over?"

"Done," Gorman replied.

"They all seemed so happy. Guess the only ones who get screamed at is Jolene and me." I stood up from the kitchen table and walked away in silence.

Roderick sighed, "I see she's still sensitive about being corrected the other day. Guess we have some damage control to contend with for her too."

Gorman nodded, "She tough on the outside, but she has a tender heart that is easily hurt."

Going to our bedroom, I passed through and made my way to the balcony. I stood at the railing and gazed out over the pool and surrounding property. The air was cool, and a light breeze blew against my skin. It was quiet and the full moon shone brightly. I felt so alone. I thought of my life before Ken Parks and all of the things I had been through.

Gorman walked up behind me and wrapped his arms around me. "You're freezing," he whispered. He wasn't good at apologies and Roderick's observation of damage control came to his mind. "I don't want to lose you, Jasmin." He stared out at the moon. "You are my light in this dark world, baby. You saved my soul." I turned to face him. He wiped away a tear as it ran down my cheek and gave me a gentle kiss. "Let's go in, It's chilly out here."

Billy pulled me onto the bed with him, covering us up with the covers. His lips caressed my neck seductively, hands slowly removing my clothing. He was passionate and we made love, taking my breath away. I fell asleep in his arms, easing the loneliness in my mind.

A couple of days later Darius announced over breakfast that he was taking the day off. He was taking Jolene to her first doctor's appointment. Then, they would go to lunch and spend the rest of the day shopping for their new addition to the family.

Gorman left for the casino. Without Jolene, it seemed weird. The house was quiet and empty. I sat by the pool in the morning sun, sipping coffee, lost in thought. I stood up, restless, pacing.

Roderick stepped out and spoke up, "Hey, you bored? We can take a ride and have lunch with Billy at the casino if you want."

"Really?", I asked suspiciously.

"You look like you need to get out of here for a while." Roderick (Kevin) was trying to fix the damage control from the Lake Mead incident.

Roderick took me to the casino and disappeared while Gorman and I ate. I was acutely aware that ununiformed security was at almost every table surrounding us. The boss was relaxed and joking. He playfully stole a bite of salad from my plate, blaming it on the waiter, who was flustered and then smiled when he realized he was just ribbing him.

When the meal was done, Gorman nodded to one of the security guards. Perfectly timed, Roderick stood at the table and the other tables around us emptied.

Sitting in the car to leave, Roderick questioned, "So how was lunch?"

"It was nice. Billy was in a good mood and the food was delicious."

We pulled out of the parking lot. Roderick sighed, "I've been meaning to talk to you. The rest of the staff at the house do not know our secret about my being Kevin or my role in the organization. I need you to keep this between us and say nothing to them."

"Ok. I can do that."

"Good. Keep it close to the vest, Jas."

"I suppose we have to go back to the house now, right?

Roderick grinned at me and winked. "Kevin knows a place we can go and have some fun."

He drove us to a small town not far away. He pulled up to a seedy strip club. The parking lot was filled with motorcycles and half a dozen beat up cars. The neon sign was almost all burned out. "You've got to be kidding me," I gasped.

"This establishment belongs to the organization. It's safe, and don't judge a book by the cover, Jasmine. Let's go let our hair down."

I groaned as he led the way. From the outside it appeared to be a roach filled dive. I squinted against the bright sun, wishing we had gone back to the Gorman estate. I was so close to Roderick's back that I ran into him as he crossed the threshold. Several voices rang out in unison, "Kevin!", they greeted.

The stage had two women stripping and swinging around on the pole. A dozen or so large, tattooed men in motorcycle club jackets sat at the tables cheering them on, and guzzling beer. The music was thumping.

All eyes turned to us as we entered. The bartender shouted out across the room, "What are you doing here in the daylight hours, Kevin? We were starting to think you were a vampire, baby. What are you drinking, your usual?"

She poured a glass of gin and slid it down the top of the bar at us. "Kevin!", two men called from the pool tables, "Come on over here you scoundrel and let us win back that money you took from us last time! And who's that honey you brought with you?"

I stepped behind him, grasping Roderick's arm for protection. "Come over here missy and we'll talk about the first thing that pops up," he shouted, several of the bikers laughing with him.

The bartender's face scrunched up and she asked, "Who do you have with you, Kevin? Aren't you going to introduce us?"

Roderick laughed, "Come on darling, you know you're my only one."

"What a bullshitter you are!", the woman jeered.

Roderick turned and addressed the crowd loudly, "Everyone, I want you to meet Jasmine, Billy Gorman's girl." Mouths flopped open and the place went silent. I squeezed in even closer to Roderick, not sure what was going on.

One of the bikers approached us and said, "You're bringing Billy's girl in here with you? What going on Kevin?"

"Yeah, and I want you to make her feel welcome, understand?"

The was a long pause. "Well," the bartender asked softly, "What are you drinking, Jasmine?"

The strippers went back to work on the pole and the music began playing again. I was so uncomfortable. Kevin took my hand, and spoke tenderly, "These are all good people, Jas, trust me when I tell you, you won't have any problems here. We are here to have fun."

The bartender repeated, "What do want, sweetie?"

"Just a soda," I replied sheepishly.

She grinned, "One rum and coke coming up."

Kevin leaned in close to my ear. "Relax. Let's shoot some pool. This is **my** bar. I have five bucks that says you can't beat me."

"Don't listen to him", the biker with a pool cue chuckled, "He's a shark, I tell you."

Kevin rolled up his sleeves and pulled away from my grip, going towards the table and leaving me exposed. "Come on, Jasmine," Kevin encouraged, "Lets roll these guys out of some cash."

In this dark and seedy bar, everyone knew Kevin was third in command. He was king here and they all loved him. They laughed, joked, and treated us both warmly. The strippers came over on their break and made small talk, even showing me a couple of moves. I was welcome and included. I took a big drink of rum and coke, picking up a pool cue.

Jolene and Darius came home early but disappeared to their quarters. Roderick was taking care of some of the household duties when Gorman came home at the end of the day. He greeted the boss, "Rosita made dinner and it's in the oven waiting on you. She was a little under the weather, so I sent her to her quarters."

"Is she ok?"

"I think so. Just a cold. Jolene and Darius have retired to their quarters as well. They had a very full day today. All is doing fine with Jolene's pregnancy."

"Good, where's Jasmine?"

"Ah, here she comes now."

I danced into the kitchen and put my arms around Billy's neck. "Hi," I grinned, kissing him softly. The boss furrowed his brow.

"Jasmine Grant, where have you been? You taste like booze and smell like cigars. Did he take you downtown to another casino?"

"Nope," I answered twirling to the music in my head that no one else could hear. "We went to the club."

"A club?", he inquired sternly, turning to stare Roderick down.

"Yeah, Kevin's bar", I whispered, dancing out of the room.

Gorman froze and turned to Roderick with fire in his eyes. "You did NOT take Jasmine to the Kitty Kat Club, did you, Kevin?" He shrugged evasively. "Look, I know you've been seeing one of the strippers down there, but that is no place for a lady!", he scolded.

"You put me in charge of the girls, did you not, Gorman?"

"I don't believe you, Kevin! You're giving me a fucking ulcer!"

"Look, boss, she needed this."

"To go to the Kitty Kat Club?"

"The Kitty Kat Club is our private club, Billy. Nobody allowed in except a select handful of our best and trusted guys. The Demons motorcycle club was there and a few of our tried and true. No rowdies, no chance of anyone from New York. Every person in the place knew she was your girl and that meant hands off. They treated her with respect. We shot pool, played darts, had a lot of laughs and a few drinks. We had an interesting conversation, and out the door. She needed to relax and have fun. She can't be locked up in this house day after day, living in fear. She needed a mental health day to let her hair down. Trust me, Billy. I not only have to protect her health, but her mind and spirit too. The girls loved her, and they even gave her some tips on pole dancing. It was good for her, Billy."

"You're fucking killing me," the boss spat, flustered at the thought. What had been done, was done. Nothing he could do about it now. Gorman shook his head and chased after Jasmine to make sure she was ok.

He caught up with Jasmine in the media room, dancing to music alone. "I can't believe he took you there," Gorman growled.

"Oh, it was wonderful, Billy! The bartender is so funny. She told jokes. The girls are so talented and really know how to dance. They took me under their wings, and we became great friends. And oh, my goodness, the Demons shoot a mean game of pool. Kevin beat them every game and they kept saying he was cheating, but we all knew he didn't. What a day!"

The boss saw a glow in Jasmine's eyes. He dropped his head in defeat, leading her to the kitchen for dinner.

The next morning, Darius and Jolene came bouncing into the kitchen. I sat at the table nursing a coffee. Gorman was looking through paperwork. Roderick was munching on an English muffin. "Guess what?", my sister burst, flashing a huge diamond ring on her finger. "Darius asked me to marry him yesterday! It was so romantic. We were in the garden of the Bellagio after watching the water show. He got down on one knee and everything!" She was gushing, her cheeks red with excitement.

The boss grunted. "That's wonderful," I said, kicking him under the table.

"So, what did you do yesterday?', Jolene asked, sipping orange juice.

"I went to lunch with Billy and…." Roderick gave me a harsh stink- eye and shook his head no, for me to be silent. "And then I just hung around here with Roderick," I replied carefully. He winked at me as Gorman gave a fake cough.

"Darius and I would like to have the wedding here, if that's ok with you, Billy. Security would be better than at the casino." She flashed a big toothy grin, begging for permission. He did not respond.

"We're keeping it small. Only about 75. I think we have the ability to handle that." Still no reply. "Billy?"

"These books are off," he mumbled under his breath.

Barrington repeated, "Gorman, the wedding- can we host it here?"

Billy looked up slowly from his paperwork. He laughed, "Of course you can. I'm just pulling your chain. This is obviously the best option." He winked at Jolene playfully, and she leapt to her feet with joy. Things were moving at light speed for Jolene and Darius.

CHAPTER 6

Jolene picked out the most beautiful wedding gown. It was an off the shoulder gown with a princess cut. The bodice was laced and beaded. The full skirt sparkled, and she was gorgeous in it, with a matching veil. It brought me to tears to see her in it.

They set the date for 5 weeks out. Rosita bustled with the menu and food preparation. Roderick became very familiar with the restrictive guest list, and everyone became involved with designing a fantastic outdoor backdrop for the ceremony, with details to include an inside reception in Gorman's ballroom. Much to the relief, there was silence from the Winter/Aguzzi organization. Jolene and I stayed close and took no chances. We had learned our lesson.

Jolene's morning sickness had begun, and we had to plan around these events. We had experts that had passed Roderick's background check come in for floral, live band, and other services to make sure the wedding was a success. It was an exciting time; filled with hope and promise for the future and filled with love.

As we were going over the guest list one afternoon with Roderick, he explained who everyone was that we might not be familiar with, giving us detailed backgrounds on Barrington's list. Jolene took the invitation list from Roderick and hand wrote a name down on it. Roderick looked at her addition, shaking his head. "I don't know about this. I need to get approval from both Gorman and Barrington, Jolene."

She raised her eyebrows at him. "Isn't it my wedding too? I only invited one person; I don't think that is too much to ask."

Roderick groaned, "I will run it past them, that's the best I can do."

With all of the preparations and hubbub, the 5 weeks flew by so quickly and soon it was the big day. Jolene and Darius both had butterflies in their stomach and were scared to death. Only Billy and I had been chosen to stand up with them and the minister. The ceremony was to be simple and fairly quick, but we practiced it for days, including the handwritten vows they had created.

Billy and Darius got ready in the Barrington wing, while Jolene and I got dressed in the main house. I stared at my reflection in the mirror. The lavender gown we had picked out was beautiful. Jolene sighed, "I didn't sleep a wink last night. I am so nervous. I'm never going to be able to cover these bags under my eyes," she chuckled.

"You look absolutely stunning," I encouraged, "And everything is going to be perfect. It's almost time". She fidgeted in her chair, brushing her hair for the 10th time. "Relax."

"I think I'm going to be sick," she grumbled.

There was a knock on the door. Roderick stuck his head inside. "You two look fabulous," he grinned. "Time for your big entrance." She nodded, swooning slightly.

"Ok. Let's go."

"I can't. I'm too nervous."

"Suck it up," I spat, "let's go!" I laughed, grabbing her hand and pulling her out the door. I took a deep breath and walked out into the garden and down the marked path. The guests were lined up on both sides of the aisle, all awaiting Jolene. My heart was pounding with the excitement and kept my eyes straight ahead on Billy and Darius waiting patiently at the altar. I focused on not tripping and looking clumsy.

The guys looked so handsome in their tuxedos. A lump formed in my throat, and I forced it down, not wanting tears to ruin my makeup. This was a wedding, not a goth concert I giggled to myself. Billy stared straight ahead as if he was nervous too. Why? I didn't know. It wasn't like HE was the one getting married.

I took my place, and the wedding march began to play. All the guests rose and turned to see the bride. As she came into view, Barrington's chest puffed out and tears welled up in his eyes as emotion swept over him. Gorman looked like a cat about to be dipped into a tub of water. "She's beautiful," Darius whispered, smiling wide. She took her place by his side as the minister began to speak. I glanced at the boss who stood there stiff and cold.

All sounds went silent in my mind, and all I could hear was my own voice saying, "Gorman seems pissed off. I wonder what I did this time. He won't even look at me."

My brain snapped back, and I heard the minister say, "I now pronounce you man and wife. You may kiss your bride." Darius and Jolene embraced with a long, sensuous kiss. They turned to the guests, the sounds of clapping and cheers. They slowly walked to the ballroom to form the reception line. Gorman did not say one word to us, only greeting the visitors with a reserved handshake. Was he worried about security? Was there an unknown threat I should be aware of?

Then I saw him. As he approached us, I jumped up and down in place. He passed us a large friendly grin. He held out his arms. Jolene and I both jumped into his arms as he gave a chuckle and squeezed us tight.

"Joseph," I gushed, "I'm so glad you made it!"

"Are you kidding? I wouldn't miss this for the world. You two look dynamite. How are you? Are these two taking good care of you? You know my offer is always open."

Barrington cleared his throat. We released his neck and fell in line at Barrington's silent command. He offered his hand to Darius, a little boy grin on his face, eyes shining in a challenge. Jolene elbowed her new husband gently and he took the US Marshall's hand in slow motion. Joseph Landry smiled, "I won't stay long. I just wanted to come by and say congratulations to the new bride and groom. I think I make your guests a little uneasy." He took great delight in that statement, laughing out loud. A low rumble came from Gorman's throat, his first sound of the day. Perhaps this was why he seemed upset.

There was no love lost between these men. The guys were aware that Joseph had tried several times to get us to turn on them and join witness protection.

My sister crooked her finger at Joseph and pulled him in close to her ear. He leaned in, a devilish smirk directly at Barrington. "I'm going to have a baby," Jolene whispered.

"That's wonderful, sweetheart." Joseph Landry kissed her tenderly on the forehead, while both Darius and Billy glared evilly at him. "I really should go now," Landry stated, feeling the heat from the men. I hugged him tight once more as Billy shifted his feet in a very irritated manner.

Gorman tipped his head and suddenly Roderick stood at Joseph's side. "Landry has to leave now, please show him out."

Joseph plucked two red roses from a large floral arrangement nearby. He handed one of them to Jolene and one to me. "For innocence desired," he said softly. Roderick folded his arms across his chest, as Landry cackled, winking playfully at us. Roderick turned and trailed Landry close behind, as Joseph made his way to the exit. Landry quickly snapped up a glass of champagne and raised it to the numerous hostile eyes, swilling it down arrogantly in one gulp. Laughing, he walked out. Just outside of view, he turned to Roderick and whispered, "We're on the same team, you and me. We have to protect the girls, Kevin." Roderick squared his shoulders at him, enraged that the US Marshall knew about his cover. It made him uneasy. What else did that damn Marshall know? Landry winked at him, again cackling as he got in his car to leave.

"I can't stand that guy," Gorman sneered, as the rest of the guests began lining up to greet Jolene and Darius. The line cleared and Billy and

I stood alone for a moment. Roderick stomped up to me with purpose, a sharp glare in his eye.

In a low tone, he demanded, "Did you two tell him I am Kevin?"

My eyes grew wide with fear. "Hell no! Why would we do that?!"

"He knows," Kevin snarled softly.

"I swear to you, we never told him a thing!", I pleaded.

"If I find out otherwise," he threatened, stepping back and locking eye contact with the boss.

Billy defended, "He's been digging, Kevin. I'm not surprised. I do not believe the girls are responsible." Roderick stormed away.

I snared Billy's arm and squeezed, "We didn't tell him." The boss uncurled my grip from his forearm and walked away in silence. I sighed and lowered my head, following him drudgingly.

The food was delicious. Rosita really out did herself. Billy barely ate, spending all of his time in secret meetings behind closed doors.

Darius and Jolene were center stage, entertaining the guests. The band started playing and they danced together, followed by the guests. Everyone was having a great time. But then, it suddenly hit me that Gorman had been purposely avoiding me all day. The wedding was nearly over, and he hadn't spoken a word to me or sat next to me, or even danced with me.

They cut the cake and I sat pushing my piece from side to side on my plate, sulking. I retreated to the bathroom and broke down. Only Jolene noticed my tears upon leaving the table.

Gorman was dancing with a guest when Jolene tapped her on the shoulder. "May I cut in?", she asked sweetly.

The woman replied, "For the bride? Of course, dear!"

"How are you doing?", the boss questioned.

Jolene responded, "I have to talk to you, Billy. I'm begging of you to please not ruin my wedding."

Gorman cocked his head to one side and gave her an inquisitive look. "What's going on Jolene?"

45

"Darius said on my wedding day you can't refuse a sincere request from the bride. I really didn't want to ask you for anything, Billy, you've been so accommodating for me and Darius. But I have to ask a favor of you."

Billy groaned, rolling his eyes. "Wasn't the favor letting that idiot Landry in here with his smug grin; cocky and snickering? I granted you that, remember?"

"This is bigger."

"Bigger?" The boss hesitated. What could possibly be bigger than that? "Fuck, Jolene," he grumbled, "What do you want of me now?"

"It's Jasmine, Billy."

"Yeah, what about her?"

They continued to slow dance. She paused, teary eyed, and pleaded, "I know that you don't love Jasmine the way Darius and I love each other. Marriage, children…But Billy, you have treated her like she has wedding cooties. Everybody knows you don't want to settle down and all, but people are talking shit about her and it's driving me crazy. I caught her crying in the bathroom."

"What do you mean they're talking shit about her?", he froze for a minute.

"They are whispering that you're ignoring her today because she's really just your whore and not your girlfriend."

"Who said that?", Gorman demanded sharply.

"It doesn't matter. The point is, I would really appreciate it if you at least danced once with her to shut these jerks up."

The music ended and the band announced they were taking a break before their last set. Jolene stared at the floor and spun around to leave in silence. Gorman snared her wrist and gazed into her heartbroken eyes. He glanced over his shoulder to see where Jasmine sat alone in the corner. Cooties, he thought. Wedding cooties. He realized that he had indeed been avoiding her and giving her the cold shoulder all day. "I'll take care of it," Billy said as Jolene departed to go be with Barrington.

The boss strolled up to Roderick. "Conference, now. Follow me." They disappeared into the empty garden area outside. Workers were feverishly taking down the altar and chairs.

"Something wrong?", Roderick questioned. "You seem agitated. Still pissed off at Landry?"

"Have you heard rumors of people talking garbage about Jasmine, that's she nothing more than my whore?" Roderick stiffened, silent. "Have you?", he pushed.

"There is some speculation, and from the look on your face, I don't think right now is the time for naming names. Why?"

"Jolene used her bride's request card."

"Which can't be denied," Roderick sighed.

"She wants me to put an end to the gossip." Roderick nodded that he understood. "She said Jasmine has been upset."

"Devasted," he answered frankly. "So, what are you thinking?"

"I'm going to kill some cooties." Billy Gorman turned and walked away.

"Cooties?", Roderick pondered aloud. "What the hell is cooties?"

The band returned to the stage. Gorman approached the stage and demanded the microphone. He glanced about the room, full of silent guests. Harshly, he spoke into the microphone, "Jasmine, get up here."

I reluctantly got to my feet. My heart sank in dread. Now he was going to publicly chastise me for some worthless infraction. As I approached, a knot formed in my stomach.

He looked down at me and I could tell he was angry over something. The crowd was hushed, anxious to see the show. He paused, lowering the microphone for a moment to collect his thoughts. I wanted to run, to burst out in tears and beg forgiveness for whatever it was I had done this time.

Billy spoke loudly into the microphone. "Some people here have decided to wag their tongues about us and open their mouth when they don't know a damn thing." I shrunk at his anger, waiting for the ax to fall. "You know I love you, right Jasmine?" He spit it out like it was nasty tasting. I was stunned. Silent. Cowering before him. "Play a damn song," he sneered, tossing the microphone on the stage. He took me in his arms and kissed me. Not a light peck on the cheek. A long, slow full tongue invasion that brought out a strong sexual desire in me. When he was done, I gasped for air, weak in the knees. The silence of the audience showed that they were fully aware of Gorman's frustration. Not one soul dared to join us on the dance floor as the music began and we started to waltz. The boss had spoken, and they knew better than to intrude on his moment.

Jolene collapsed back in her chair with a sigh of relief. Darius and Roderick both folded their arms across their chests. Let no one deny this announcement. Jolene watched Jasmine and Billy very intimately waltzing alone on the dance floor. She laughed, "Fuck yeah." Both men turned to her to scold her vulgarity. Her eyes gleamed. She was the bride, and the situation as it was, they repeated her sentiments with a playful grin.

Guests quickly began to depart, not taking a chance of Gorman's wrath falling upon them for starting rumors and bashing Jasmine. It was awkward and they ran like scared dogs.

CHAPTER 7

The wedding had been so beautiful and perfect, despite wagging tongues and an awkward moment with US Marshall Landry. Darius surprised Jolene with a 2-week European excursion for their honeymoon. It included several countries and cities. A whirlwind of excitement and romance. She was ecstatic and they flew out that very night.

With Darius and Jolene gone, the house was so quiet and empty. Billy worked long hours to cover for Barrington's absence. I sulked; bored and stared blankly at the television for days. One afternoon Roderick and I slipped away to Kevin's bar. It was always so much fun and inviting there. Gorman still wasn't fond of the idea, though. Kevin always checked before we got there to make sure it was secure and had plenty of armed guards for our protection.

I was very happy when Barrington and Jolene returned from their honeymoon. We sat talking for hours. A few days after they got back, Billy gave Roderick the day off. He needed a break from the responsibility of guarding my sister and me. He seemed relieved. (And I knew he wanted to see a particular stripper from the Kitty Kat Club, but I kept that knowledge to myself.)

Jolene had another doctor's appointment that afternoon and the plan was that Billy and Darius would work for only a short part of the day. Then we would all go to lunch. After lunch Darius and Jolene would go to the appointment, and Gorman and I would actually get to spend a little time together at the house. I was giddy when we entered the casino. Four of the boss's guards surrounded us for protection, hovering over us as we gambled a little. Gorman and Barrington disappeared to handle some business. It was a magical feeling of comfort.

10:00 AM - Jolene and I had both been on a losing streak on the casino floor. We thought we would take a break and go grab a soda at the snack bar. I was handing the cashier money to pay for the soda when suddenly the fire alarms sounded, and the casino began to fill with smoke.

The alarms were blaring, piercing my ears. Parts of the casino floor were not visible due to thick smoke. Customers began to panic and run for the exits, as the guards began herding them to safety. There was a massive push towards the door and in the rush and confusion, Jolene and I started looking for the guys in the faces of the crowd. Jolene cried out as a couple of elderly patrons fell from being pushed and was in the process of being trampled. "Help her!", Jolene cried out to our remaining 2 guards. The security detail rushed to the elderly victim's aid, helping several people to their feet, and diverting any more of the stampeding customers. With their arms around the fallen and injured, we watched as they made their way to the front doors.

Jolene began coughing and choking over the now blinding smoke. My eyes were burning, and I had the feeling of being disoriented as to where the exits were located. "We have to get out of here, Jolene. Darius and Billy will catch up to us, but we need fresh air!"

In the smoke and confusion, there was a sudden rush of firemen filtering the casino. They were assisting customers and disbursing, looking for the location of the flames. We started for a nearby exit, when one of the firemen in full face mask and carrying a fire ax called out to us, "Ma'am! Ma'am! You can't use that exit! Flames have compromised the integrity of the access." He made his way over to us. "The captain says that the fire is spreading across that area of the casino fast. Follow me to this alternate exit and I will guide you to safety."

Jolene was really starting to cough hard. The fireman motioned over another firefighter and the two of them slid the oxygen masks over Jolene and me. Tears streaked down my face from the smoke. Nearly blinded by inhalation, the kind firefighters took us gently by the arm and led us through the dense smoke. My ears were ringing from the blasting overhead alarms and we followed them blindly towards the exit.

We were near the exit door when I began to feel woozy and lightheaded from the oxygen and stress. A sense of fear settled in, as my knees became weak. My head was spinning, and I collapsed in the firefighter's arms. He lifted me up in a fireman's carry and easily threw me up over his shoulder. The oxygen was at full blast, and yet, I passed out and everything went dark. The last thing I saw was Jolene stumbling to the floor and being scooped up by the other fireman.

I was in the twilight, not awake, not asleep. The burning and stinging of my eyes subsided and I struggled to see against the mask on my face. The bright light of the sun made me bury my face against the back of the firefighter's thick jacket. We were safe. We were out of the casino. Out of the fire and smoke. Yet, I was limp and unable to move. My limbs were as lead and my voice could not speak.

There was the jostling of being carried. Steps up into an …ambulance? Firetruck? A house? The firemen softly placed me on a soft seat. A couch? What? It began moving as my head was spinning and I started to vomit. "Cut the ether. Switch to oxygen," a voice thundered. My mask was replaced, and I was no longer swooning. My ears stopped ringing. My eyes cleared of the burning. I breathed the oxygen in deep and no longer gagged and gasped for air. "Good job. Dump the uniforms and let's get out of here. Drive slowly, we don't want to attract any attention."

Everything lifted from my brain. I was slumped over on a couch in an RV motor home. And we were moving! Jolene sat next to me, groaning, "Oh, I'm gonna be sick. Jasmine."

"It's ok. I'm here," I mumbled in a clearing fog.

"Andiamo! Andiamo!"

I sat up like a shot, leaping to my feet. My legs did not hold me, and I crumpled into a pile on the couch, not able to sit or stand. There was a haunting sound of laughter that filled my ears. Agguzi's menacing face came into view. He grabbed a handful of my hair and violently man handled my limp body into a sitting position.

Jolene sat up on her own and sneered, "What the hell??"

"I suggest you make no sudden movement until the effects of the sleeping gas wear off, or you could hurt yourself."

I snapped my eyes open and turned my head to the left. Trent Winter sat in a swivel chair smugly glaring at me. Jolene made a weak attempt to kick and fight Aguzzi, collapsing onto the floor in a heap, unable to fully move her extremities.

"Why do they never listen?" Winter chuckled. "Help her up, Sal." He picked her up and slammed her down like a rag doll on the seat.

"So, we meet again," Aguzzi growled evilly.

I gathered my strength and in slow motion made it to my feet, attempting to make it to the door. Winter drew his gun and pointed it at me. "Sit down, Jasmine. You're not going anywhere." I halted but did not sit. "Sal," he addressed his henchman, "how long do you think she can stand with a bullet in each kneecap? 40 seconds? Maybe a minute?"

"If she's lucky and doesn't pass out from the pain.", Aguzzi mused.

"You want to find out, Jasmine?" I glared into his eyes with defiance. "I said sit. I don't like repeating myself. Maybe I'll just start with her." He turned the gun onto my helpless sister. He cocked the hammer, firing a shot directly above her head and blowing a small bullet hole all the way through the wall. "I'm not Parks. You'll only get 1 warning shot out of me, Jasmine."

I tumbled to the couch. I knew Winter enough to know he didn't bluff. The RV had made it onto the highway and the road was flying under us as we left the city. "Let us go," Jolene demanded, now able to sit on her own.

Sal chuckled, "Not likely, missy."

Trent Winter and I locked eyes. "You have to let Jolene off of this bus," I muttered. Winter stared right through me, saying nothing. "Did you hear me? I said you have to let Jolene off of this bus, damn it!" All I could think about was that Jolene was pregnant. It created terror inside of me. What would become of the baby at the hands of their torcher?

Trent snickered hideously, his lips curling into a mocking grin. He aimed the gun back at me.

Jolene whispered, "It's ok, Jasmine. Sit down and shut up. I'm ok."

There was an innocent child growing inside of her. A baby that never asked for this mob war. A life that was so fragile and could be snubbed out so easily. I repeated tenderly, "You have to let her go, Winter."

His eyes narrowed on me; lips pursed tight. He stared intensely at me. "Interesting," he thought out loud, evaluating my request.

"When Darius finds us, he's going to fucking kill you, assholes.", Jolene growled.

Winter turned to her. "No, he won't, Jolene. You see those precious tracking devices that they count on so much are worthless. This RV has been equipped with a jamming system. You know what they are reading on you two right now? Nothing! Fucking static."

He was cocky, arrogant, and smug. I knew from his demeanor, that what he said was 100 % true. I closed my eyes and sighed sadly. "Let her go, Winter."

"My, you are persistent, aren't you, Jasmine?" He stood and walked with purpose to the couch I sat on. He grabbed my face in his palm firmly, sneering, "Why? Why is it so important to you she gets off this bus?"

Jolene quickly responded, "Jasmine, shut up. It's ok. Fuck him. He can eat shit!"

Trent Winter tipped his head deep to the side. A smirk of amusement gave way to a sinister look that turned his face to stone. "Really?", he said coldly. "Sal, cut her tongue out."

"With pleasure," Sal flooded, so eager to do the deed and wallow in the blood. He protruded a huge knife, coming across the RV at a quick pace.

"No!" I screamed in horror. "Let her go, and I will cooperate with you."

Winter's attention snapped back at me, "What? Oh, you'll cooperate with me?" he threatened.

Jolene pleaded desperately, "Jasmine, no, you can't. Gorman will kill you."

"You need me to break the code on the disk."

"Jasmine, no."

Winter seemed intrigued, "The great Jasmine Grant suddenly wants to negotiate with me now?" He was snide and cruel. "Tell me why you want her out."

"Let her go and I will give you full cooperation."

Sal was at Jolene's throat with the knife, ready to perform his task, "Wait!", Trent barked sternly. "I'm growing impatient with you, Jasmine! I won't ask you again. Are you trying to piss me off?"

"She's pregnant," I cried.

"Pregnant?", Winter cackled harshly.

Sal laughed, "That's ok. I can take care of that too!" He pressed the tip of the blade into Jolene's abdomen taunting her with hideous pleasure.

I leapt to my feet, screaming, "It'll be the last thing you ever do, mother fucker. I will hunt you down and kill you myself!"

In moments, there was screaming and yelling as Jolene, Salvatore, and myself all started leveling threats at each other in a deafening roar inside the RV.

Trent rubbed his temple with his free hand and shouted, "The next person to fucking speak, I'm going to shoot you in the head!" His tone was low and matter of fact, silencing the chaos. The RV rolled on in silence, not wanting to be the one Winter shot.

"Sit down," Trent ordered me, and I flopped to the couch lifeless, in submission. He pointed to Aguzzi. "You, shut up and take your seat over there!" Jolene was sobbing in silence. With the situation under control, Winter placed the firearm in his shoulder holster and pressed his fingertips together in deep thought. What seemed like an eternity passed as he pondered this new information.

Winter studied me intently, eyes burning through my very soul. I wanted to scream out at the top of my lungs, I wanted to curse, I wanted to beg for mercy. I wanted out of this RV.

I closed my eyes, shoulders slumping, and I dropped my head, hiding the building tears in the corners of my eyes. For the first time, I didn't have a plan, and I didn't know what to do.

A deep belly laugh rolled out of Winter's mouth. "Well, fuck!" he commented sarcastically. Gritting my teeth, I glared at him. This was no laughing matter, bastard.

I felt no hope of mercy. Groomed by Ken Parks to be vicious beyond measure, Trent Winter was as evil and cruel as they came. We didn't stand a chance of getting out of this alive. His eyes burned through me, intense and hardened. I attempted a defiant return gaze, only to slip in bravery and pleading desperately. "Please," I whispered.

He retrieved the gun in his hand. "Did I not say for everyone to shut up while I sort this out?" He was annoyed, frustrated, and angry at the whole lot of us. He pointed the barrel of the handgun at my forehead. The 45 looked like a canon to me.

"What do you want of me?", I questioned in a hollow tone. He was quiet, mulling things over in his mind. "It's not just about us anymore, Winter. We're talking about an innocent life here."

"Jasmine, no! Don't you do it," Jolene hissed. "You can not cooperate with this asshole. Do you know what Billy will do to you? No!"

A grin appeared on Trent's lips. "She's right you know. Gorman will kill you for betraying him."

"That's a chance I have to take. He will have to understand I'm trying to save the baby here. An innocent life. We were innocent once."

Trent put the gun back in its holster once more as the miles rolled on. Tension was through the roof, as no one spoke a word. Sal lowered the knife, waiting for Winter's instructions and Jolene pegged him the finger in defiance.

Trembling, I stood up and approached where Winter was sitting. I knelt on the floor before him. "Let her go. I will cooperate with you 100 %. I'll give you the access code to the disk. Isn't that what you really want?" A knot was in my throat, and I was choked up in terror.

He leaned back in the seat. "I can get that code out of you, whether you cooperate or not, Jasmine."

"You'll try. But I will die first if you don't accept my offer."

"Is that a threat?"

"No," I sighed. "It's the truth."

He squared his shoulders at me and leaned forward, close to me in an intimidating manor. He quickly gazed at the rest of the occupants in the RV. After a moment, he said flatly, "This is what's going to happen. I'll do a prisoner swap. Salvatore for you." He turned to his henchman, who now seemed quite unhappy with this proposal. "Sal, you have a new mission. You take Jolene back to Barrington. Safely. Unharmed, do you understand me? Jasmine stays. Sal is Gorman's prisoner, Jasmine is mine."

A flood of protests erupted from everyone's mouth. "No," Sal spat. "Gorman and Barrington will kill me."

"Anything happens to you, Aguzzi, I ship her back to him one piece at a time. Jolene will see they treat you like a king. Or else."

"I don't like this, boss," Aguzzi muttered.

"Did I ask you?", Trent commanded. "When Jasmine has completed her task here, I will return her to Gorman, and we will make the swap. When I get the information from the disk, I will in turn take Jolene and the child out of the game. This is a very generous offer, Jasmine, and it will not be repeated. Do we have an agreement?"

His eyes burned through my soul. This was my only chance of saving the baby.

"Jasmine," Jolene whispered, "the price is too high. Darius and I can have another child."

"What do you say, Jasmine?", Winter was pushy and cold.

I closed my eyes, filled with pain. "Deal," I sighed.

Aguzzi cackled, "And she makes a deal with the devil."

Jolene cried softly, "Jasmine, no."

"It's done," Trent ordered. "Next rest stop, Aguzzi and Jolene are out." He pointed to Jolene with a menacing pointer finger, "you tell Barrington, he better take good care of my man here. Or else."

The RV pulled into the very next rest area. Jolene and Sal stepped out and Jolene instantly started to call Darius to come and get her.

I sputtered, "I can give you the code right now, Trent. Then I can go with Jolene, and you can take Sal with you. No worries. I can give you the code right now."

"You volunteered for this Jasmine. I'm not done with you yet. This is on my terms now. Driver – go."

The door closed and we pulled away. My sister and the baby were safe, but at what cost? The driver questioned, "Same destination, Mr. Winter?"

"We stick with the plan."

"Do you need one of us to stay back here with you to watch the girl?"

Trent's jaws locked tight. "No. I have this. After all, she's going to be in total compliance, right Jasmine? Make sure the signal scrambler is active. I don't' need Gorman rushing in for the rescue." The RV picked up speed and continued on its sadistic journey.

CHAPTER 8

I was silent, resting my head in my hands. I felt weak and defeated. "Now, now," Trent said across the RV from his chair. "Why are you sulking? Haven't I shown you I can be reasonable? Surely this doesn't have to end in another bloody massacre, Jasmine. Let me get us a drink and put some music on." He poured two glasses and turned on some calming music. He passed me a glass of rum and closed his eyes. "Music soothes the soul, don't you think?"

"I just want this over."

"Mmmm….so hostile. Patience, Jasmine. All in due time."

The sun was starting to set as we drove, surrounded by empty desert. A good place to dump a body, I thought. The dirt road we were traveling on was isolated. A large building came into sight. It looked like maybe it had been an old warehouse, abandoned now, and very remote. The overhead door rose, and the RV drove into the building, the door closing down behind us. I squirmed uncomfortably. Again, I thought it would be a place to leave a body with none the wiser.

The driver stepped into the back with us. "Location is secure, Mr. Winter. Signal blocker is engaged. RV is surrounded and they have all been filled in with your instructions."

"Do you like pizza?", Winter asked. I shrugged, rolling my eyes up in my head. "Well, I'm hungry," Trent announced. "This might take awhile and we're going to need food. Take Tony and go get us pizza and beer for while we're working tonight." He was acting odd – smug at his win. His man disappeared, off to fulfill his boss's request.

"I don't think this will take long," I scoffed, "especially since you only have 1 of the 3 disks."

"What?", Winter demanded coldly, going from smug to angry. "What is this '3 disks' you're talking about? You mean there are more?"

My mouth flopped open. "Oh, you didn't know?" I asked sheepishly. "Great. Just great."

"Jasmine, are you breaking our agreement?", he growled, "That's not a game you want to play with me."

I ran my fingers through my hair, exhaling loudly. This was about to go badly. I held out my hands to him and had to explain how dad had made 3 disks that all had to be running together to get the full picture. Each disk was a piece of the puzzle. I thought he was going to hit the roof. His calm demeanor faded, replaced by fire in his eyes and protruding veins in his neck.

"I can't believe you fucking tricked me again!", he exclaimed, now pacing the floor. He glared in my direction haughtily and paced some more.

"I didn't trick you," I defended. "I thought Parks told you."

"Convenient you didn't divulge this until after we made our agreement," he growled.

Softly I said, "Why would I? We're enemies and this is war, right?"

He glared at me in fury, and I knew I was really pushing his buttons. The door opened and his driver entered with pizza and beer. He hadn't been gone long, so I knew there was a town or something close. Maybe I could make an escape after all. The driver could see the tension between us. "Just set it on the table," Winter instructed. The driver nodded at Trent and vanished quickly. Winter had his hands on his hips, head tilted in rage at me.

"Mmm…pizza smells good," I gulped. "I'm starving." I proceeded to open the box and pull a slice out. "So, where's your stupid disk?" I took a big bite, and with a mouth full of food, mumbled, "wow, this is great pizza," mocking him.

"You drive me fucking crazy," Trent sneered.

"Funny, Gorman says the same thing," I smiled.

He slammed the disk down on the table, then tore off a slice of pizza and chomped on it, while giving me the evil eye. I opened a beer and took a long drink, letting out a loud burp to be extra obnoxious. I was going to make this hell.

Trent regained his calm. "All right, you've had your fun, Jasmine. Time for us to go to work. This doesn't feel like 100% cooperation to me. I can still change my mind."

"Ok," I conceded. My palms began to sweat. "Put the disk in."

"What's the access code?" I hesitated. "Jasmine," he snapped," the code!"

I closed my eyes, tipping my head back and staring at the ceiling. "Here we go again. Billy and Darius stared at their screen for days, Winter. They never could figure it out. They were so damn mad. I don't want to do this, Trent." I gave a long pause. "This is a really nice camper."

"RV," he corrected. "And it should be for nine hundred and eighty-seven thousand dollars."

"Million-dollar RV. Impressive."

"Enough. You can't even imagine what I am going to do to your sister and that baby if you don't give me that fucking code right now." He stomped across the floor and grabbed my shoulders, pulling me to my feet.

I hated myself. I knew Gorman would be so furious with me. "We were innocent once," I moaned, lost in thought.

"You stopped being innocent the day you slapped Ken Parks across the face, Jasmine."

Trent Winter was good at reading people's emotions. It was his advantage. "I need you right now, sweetheart." He was quiet, inches from my face. Nobody had ever told me they needed me before. Our game of wills had played its last hand.

"M..I..T..R.. O.. A.. E", I said gently. He feverishly put the code into the computer and the screen came alive and Trent's face lit up in victory. "What kind of code is that?"

"It means money is the root of all evil."

He laughed, "Of course it does." He released his grip on me and I stumbled across the floor and fell onto the couch like a rag doll. "Where are you going?", he questioned.

"You don't need me anymore. I'm not allowed to see what the disk says."

"Is that so? Gorman's stupid rules I suppose. Well, I'm not Gorman. Get over here and help me with this." He pulled me to my feet and dragged me to the computer, sitting me down in a chair, facing the screen. He stood behind me and we stared at the screen together. He suddenly pressed himself very close to my back, smelling my hair. It was weird, awkward, and crazily, kind of sensuous. His hands slid down my shoulders seductively. I attempted to stand, to get away from him, but he held me down in the chair. "I need you to do this for me," Trent said sternly. "I am a patient man, but I have waited a long time for this", he confessed.

I had to admit that actually getting to see the screen for the disk got my heart beating fast. What was on these disks that had 2 organizations at war for the information? "Does any of this look familiar to you, Trent?" He observed over my shoulder, standing so close I became very uncomfortable. "Look. There is a list of names and dates. I have no idea what this code means. Do you?"

"Scroll down," he instructed. I did as he requested, slowly scrolling down through the list of names and dates." "Son of a bitch," he sighed, and I understood he did indeed know what this list was.

"So, are you going to share with me, Winter, or just use me and keep me hanging like Gorman and Barrington?"

"Alright. Once I tell you what this is, you will never be innocent in my eyes again, Jasmine. Are you ready for that?"

"I stopped being innocent the day Ken Parks slit my dad's throat. You know that. What is this?"

"This is a hit list, Jasmine."

"How do you know that?"

"Because I know how many of these people I took out. This is a list of all hits. I see some from all of us."

"Gorman and Barrington?"

"When I said all, I meant all. Yes. What I don't see is who ordered the hit."

"That must be on one of the disks that Billy has."

"Go to the next screen," he demanded.

I hit enter and more mystery information appeared. "What is this?". I asked.

"Money laundering. Next screen. Drugs. Names of informants. Shit! Dallas, LA, Miami, Chicago. Big and small. He has the goods on everybody." But so much was in code or missing. Strange icon on the boarder, but no idea what it meant. It was like reading a book with several missing pages- all at the most critical moment. It had to be on the other disk.

Winter pulled up a chair and sat next to me. "Tell me what you see Jasmine," he encouraged. "I know your father must've shared some of his accounting symbols with you over the years. I want to know everything."

I was caught up in the rush of discovery. I had been forbidden to see this from Darius and Billy. Didn't they trust me? Was it so I would be able to deny any knowledge in case of capture?

We stared at that laptop for hours. Winter made mental notes and even took a few handwritten observations. Before we knew it, it was 3:00 in the morning. I yawned as we continued to scroll, closing in on the end. This was so exciting, and yet somehow so draining.

Winter hit the power on the laptop and the screen went dark. "What are you doing?" I protested loudly. We're not done!"

"We need rest. We need to look at this again with fresh eyes in the morning."

"Nonsense," I yawned again, "I can keep going."

"I like your optimism," Winter grinned. "I have created a monster. Now I have to figure out what to do with you. I thought you would have been beaten to death and in a shallow grave by now." He smirked devilishly at me. Was he teasing me? Or serious?

He took my hand and led me to the back of the RV. "Just one bed," he said in a sly tone. "Looks like we're sharing. Take your clothes off." I stood immobile, heart racing. I was filled with dread, knowing that it was going to come down to this at some point. "You swore 100 % cooperation with me, Jasmine, remember?"

"I can't do that, Winter, and you know it." In desperation, I put my fists in the air, taking a boxing stance, and ready to duke it out.

He took a step back and grinned at me, "Whoa, feisty!"

"Lets just do this and get it over with," I said, tears welling up in me. "I know I am going to lose, but I am going to fight you with everything I have."

"Is that so? Well then…" Trent took a step back and raised his fists at me. I gulped.

"Hhmmm….I don't think I feel like fighting you, darling." He grabbed my hands in his, pushing them down to my sides.

"I love Billy Gorman," I pleaded.

He wrapped his arms around me and hugged me tenderly, whispering in my ear, "Of course you do. But know that when he's done playing with you, he will either toss you out like yesterday's garbage or put a bullet in your head. At that point, I am collecting his leftovers. When it's right, Jasmine, you will not be fighting me. Trust me, you will be more than willing. Kiss me."

"What? I'm not kissing you."

"Kiss me. I'm not asking. I should've taken Parks out in the very beginning. Then it would've been you and me right now – not you and Gorman. Kiss me. I want to see if you and I would be good together. Are we actually destined for each other?"

"You can't tell that from one kiss," I whispered in protest, still captured in his arms.

"Do you know the restraint I am showing you? I haven't been with a woman since Parks and I took you and Jolene."

"But you're the boss," I said quietly.

"When word got out of our brutality and what we had done to you two, no woman would go near me. They were all too terrified I might do the same to them. Up until now, you have cooperated with me per our agreement. I will not force myself on you, if you grant me this. I read people, Jasmine. It's what I do. I need to know." I hesitated. There was an intense look in his eye that this was not to be disputed. "Not a kiss like you give your long lost aunt with the whiskers growing out of her chin on Christmas. I consider it a small price to pay for your virtue. Don't you?"

He pulled me in tight to him, and I did not pull away. He placed his hands on my lower back, drawing me in seductively. His lips met mine in a tender embrace. He was gentle and inviting. He was sweet and his tongue entered my mouth. I did not fight him. His hands moved down to my rearend and pulled me into him. His kiss became engulfing and hungry. The kiss seemed to last forever and to appease his sense of curiosity and to prevent this turning into a rape, I kissed him back.

I kissed him back the way I wished I could kiss Billy. With my raw soul exposed to him. He removed his tongue from my mouth, both of us coming up breathless. I was weak in the knees. We stared into each other's eyes, both knowing that was one hell of a kiss. "We'd be dangerous together, love," he whispered, placing his forehead against mine softly, still reeling from the ecstasy. "God, I want you, "he sighed. His confession left me stunned and speechless.

He pulled me down on the bed next to him awkwardly. "Do I need to remind you that I have armed guards outside this RV? If you try to escape, they have orders to shoot to kill you and they will not hesitate."

"I gave you my word when we made the deal, Trent. Trust me." He laughed in disbelief and put his arm around me tightly to prove I was still his prisoner. I gazed at the ceiling, frozen. I wasn't sure he would keep his promise not to rape me. I did not trust him.

I awoke at 8:00 am and rolled out of the bed quietly, so not to wake Trent up. I wandered out to the computer and turned it on, rummaging through the cabinets. No food. No coffee.

Cautiously, I cracked the RV door and stood face to face with two men who had their guns drawn and pointed at my head. I held up my hands in surrender, reassuring them. "Hey, calm down. I'm not going anywhere. Look. I am going to sit down right here in this doorway on the threshold, ok? See? Not going anywhere." They were silent, guns not wavering. "I just want to talk."

"What do you want?", one of the guards interrogated harshly.

"Well," I sighed calmly, "There is no coffee or food in this camper."

"RV."

"Whatever. The boss is gonna want coffee and breakfast when he gets up. One of you stay here with their gun on me the whole time, while one goes and gets what the boss needs."

"You know nothing about what he needs."

"Can I lower my arms?" I placed my hands in my lap. "We're just talking here. I'm sure you guys need coffee too. I mean, you've been on watch all night. I gave Trent my word I would not do anything stupid, like try to escape. I am a woman of my word, but boy do I get cranky if I don't get my morning java. No coffee could really turn this into a bad day for all of us. None of us want Winter to be ugly, do we? All I am asking for is a little caffeine and a little breakfast. I will stay right here, just like this till you get back."

CHAPTER 9

I was sitting at the computer when Winter came rushing out into the living area. "What the hell are you doing?", he burst out hysterically.

"Sleep well?", I asked nonchalantly. "Don't worry. We need this information too. It's not like I am going to erase it or change anything. Have a coffee and donut and calm down. I was thinking about this icon here. Dad sometimes used this secret icon to hide a subpage underneath what you see. It goes deeper into the program. Look here – I think that is what this icon does. I was waiting for you to show you."

He ruffled his hair with his fingertips and rubbed his face to wake up. "Wait," he said abruptly, "we have no coffee."

"Yeah, we do. And donuts. I sent your guy on a supply run this morning while you were sleeping."

"You sent my men for coffee, and they left?"

"Oh, no," I explained. "Bob stayed and kept guard on me while Tom went for coffee and donuts. Don't worry. Bob held the gun on me while I sat in the doorway the whole time. We had a nice little talk. Did you know he loves baseball? He's at the opening game every year. His favorite is the chili dog with onions. His wife is a nurse and soon to retire. His oldest daughter is just about to graduate college and his youngest want to be a rock star when he grows up."

Winter gazed at me, getting a cup of coffee.

"Fucking amazing," he grumbled.

"What?", I asked innocently. "You didn't know about Bob?"

"What I know about Robert is I give him a job to do and pay him for it. That's it."

"Well, you should get to know your men. He's really nice once you get to know him." I slurped from my coffee and gazed over the rim at Trent, who seemed miffed by my encounter. He in turn, sipped from his cup- glad there was coffee for him. "Can we look at this icon now?", I asked.

Wearily, he waved his hand at me. "Sure." He took a seat next to me at the computer. "Let me ask you, Jasmine, why are you still helping me? I thought we were through after last night."

"I gave you my word I would help you. Don't besmirch my honor." He grinned, sliding in even closer to me to see the screen. "You see this tiny symbol, watch what happens when I click on it." Suddenly, a whole new set of pages and documents appeared. They had been hidden. Winter reached for a donut. "I'm not sure what this is though, Trent. This was under the hit list. There're two columns of names here. Are these more murders?"

"No. This is who ordered the hit and who took the contract."

"How do you know?" He pointed to one of the columns that had a name on it. I remember this guy. Had to shoot his dog to get to him. Coffee's good." He leaned in close to the screen. "Oh yeah, this is revealing." Suddenly he was intensely going down the list.

"You guys did all of these killings?"

"Jasmine, what did you think you would find on these disks? Tea cake recipes? This is only the ones your father knew about." So many by Parks. By Winter. Even some by Barrington. Then I started seeing Gorman. I filled with dread, scrolling down the list. Diego. Billy. Parks. Winter. Billy. Darius. It went on and on. Gorman. Gorman. Gorman.

Suddenly Trent reached for the computer to shut it down as more and more victims came on the screen. "Stop!", I screamed. "Don't you fucking touch that!" He covered the screen with an open hand.

"Jasmine, no. No more," Winter pleaded. "Shut it down. You don't want to go any further, baby." My finger impulsively hit the scroll bar one more time. Winter sighed, "I told you to shut it down."

The new information came into focus. I instantly swiveled in my seat to face him. "Why is my mother's name on this list, Winter?", I demanded. "Why is my mother's name on this list?!!" He stared at me blankly and then shut his eyes in regret, going limp in his seat and setting the coffee down on the table.

"Why didn't you stop when I asked you to?"

Tears welled up in my eyes. "This says my father put a hit out on my mother and Billy Gorman took the job. He got paid half a million dollars to kill my mom?" I gulped. Waves of emotion ran over me. Anger, sorrow, terror, disbelief, rage.

"We've all done things we weren't proud of. Taken jobs that weren't fair. I see he never told you. Perhaps that's why he agreed to protect you from Parks. Maybe he had watched you from a distance your whole life."

"You're creeping me out. Tell me this isn't true." He was silent, with a sad look in his eyes.

"Guess we're all just a bunch of assholes. Sorry you had to find out this way."

"Was my father a mobster too? Why did he want my mother dead?"

Trent took his coffee and took a long drink. Pursing his lips, he debated in his mind just how much he really wanted to reveal. "Let's just say his hands weren't clean. When you deal in our business day in and day out, you become one of us. He wanted your mother out of the way. Once she learned of his infidelity with Jolene's mom, he was afraid she would expose him and his criminal activities. Landry was hanging around even then, trying to take us all down and turn your mother."

"This can't be real," I said, heartbroken and ashamed.

"Choose to believe it or not. The disk isn't lying."

I was shattered, muttering, "Parks and your organization killed my father. Gorman and his organization killed my mother." An eerie silence filled the RV. I was numb. Horrified. And so damn angry.

Winter pulled me into his arms to comfort me. "None of us wanted you to find this out, Jasmine. You know, if you want to stay with me, I'm ok sacrificing Sal."

I pulled out of his arms. "What?" He gave me a flirty look. I scowled, "I've done everything you asked. I want to go home now, please." He closed his eyes, sighed, and nodded ok.

As the RV rode back towards Las Vegas, Winter pondered things in his mind. He now knew how to access the disk and the hidden submenus. But he only had one. Gorman had the other two. He wondered what was on Gorman's disks. He needed to find a way to get those other disks. Jasmine was the key. His plan had been to divide and conquer. It may come to fruition. He gave a half-cocked grin, gazing at Jasmine as she stared blankly in space. The disk had given him so much more than he had hoped for.

The ride home seemed to take forever. I was devastated. The RV came to a rest just outside the Gorman estate front gate. When it stopped, Trent told the driver to keep the RV running, but turn off the signal scrambler.

Trent dialed his cellphone. "Gorman, as you can see, I am here at the gate with my prisoner, ready to make the swap. Sal better be in perfect shape." Suddenly the driver and the two others joined us in the main cabin of the RV. They had AK15s in hand. Winter also took an assault weapon from a small access closet. Shit, that had been in there the whole time? I might have been able to shoot my way out of this. There was also an old guitar in the closet. My eyes met Winter's.

"This is how it's going to go down," he instructed. "They'll have guns, we'll have guns. Jasmine, you walk through that gate at the same time as Salvatore. We do the swap and drive away. Nobody gets hurt in the exchange. I'm not interested in a shoot out right now. Got it?"

"Got it."

The RV door was opened. The AK15s were pointed out the windows. My palms were sweating. The security gates opened, and I saw Gorman's limo drive up. The limo had weapons pointed out of their windows at the RV.

"Before you go, Jasmine," Trent whispered softly, "I want you to see that I'm not Ken Parks. Nobody orders me around. I play the game by my own rules. Whether I choose mercy or cruelty, that is all up to me now. Are you sure you want to go back to Gorman? We could be so good together."

I reflected back on the hot, sensual kiss of the night before, repeating his words, "We'd be dangerous together, love."

He chuckled, "Call me if you change your mind. Go now...they're waiting. Go slowly, we don't need a slaughter, do I make myself clear?"

"Yes." I stepped from the RV to the ground, acutely aware of the guns pointed at me from both directions.

Sal stepped from the limo, and we began walking slowly towards each other. The tension made me want to pass out with stress. I met Salvatore Aguzzi halfway. He stopped addressing me privately. "You ok missy?" We were both tense, knowing this could all go south and have a blood bath on our hands, with us in the crosshairs.

"I'm ok. You, ok? Gorman treat you alright?" I was terrified of the repercussions.

"Yeah," he confirmed. I breathed a sigh of relief. He tipped his head toward the RV. "Winter hurt you? Have his way with you?"

"No. He was a perfect gentleman.", I answered.

"No kidding. I'll be damned."

"Billy do anything to you?"

"No. I need a favor from you."

"A favor?" I was taken aback.

"That maid they got has the best biscuits and gravy I ever ate. You think you can get me her recipe?"

I laughed out loud at his request. "I don't know. She's pretty tight lipped about that stuff, but I will try."

Sal winked at me. "Ok. We better get moving missy, before they get itchy fingers. You know, Gorman's pretty pissed off at you. Be careful around him, girly."

"Thanks for the warning." We both continued on our paths towards our own organization. I breathed a sigh of relief as I got to the limo. The gate closed and the RV drove away.

"Get in the car," Gorman sneered. His eyes burned through me, and I knew he was hostile and filled with rage. I sat across from Billy, taking refuge next to Darius. The silence was earth shattering. But as I sat there, waiting for all hell to break loose, I thought about the disk. I thought how Billy Gorman killed my mother. At that moment, I don't know who was more livid. I grew cold.

The limo came to rest at the house. Gorman waived his hand and the guards disbanded quickly. Jolene came rushing out of the house to greet me. She gave me a big hug. "Thank God you're ok," she gushed.

As Roderick appeared from the house, Gorman snared my wrist and threw me up against the limo with force. Gorman growled, "How could you betray me with that fucking son of a bitch, Jasmine? I've spent the last year protecting you from him, risking everything for you, and you do this to me? I should kill you where you stand!"

He pulled his side arm and placed it on my temple. "You gave up the disk, didn't you?? Didn't you?? Complete cooperation? Did that include you spreading your legs for the enemy? Do you know what I have been through for you?!"

Stunned by his assault, my mouth flopped open, but no words would come out. Why couldn't I defend myself? Why didn't I scream, "you killed my mother!?", but I said nothing, tears streaming down my face, fury billowing up in my guts.

Jolene pleaded, "Billy, it wasn't like that. She did it for the baby."

Gorman pulled the hammer back, pressing the barrel hard against my skull. "We're done! We're fucking done, do you understand me?", he exploded.

What happened next, suddenly slowed down into slow motion before my eyes. Roderick pulled a weapon from the back of his belt. He placed it in the back of Gorman's head. Then Darius pulled a gun and pointed it at Roderick. Jolene burst into tears, pleading for everyone to just stop. My heart was beating wildly.

Roderick shouted, "Damn it, Gorman, you hired me to protect these girls from all comers. That means even you and Darius! Put the fucking gun down!"

The blood drained from my face. I got weak in the knees. Barrington screamed, "Damn it, Kevin! Don't make me do it! Don't make me fucking kill you! I will…."

"Darius!", Jolene cried, "Stop it. Please. Stop. Too many guns! Just stop!"

Billy lowered his gun, growling, "Get out! Get the fuck out of my house before I change my mind. We're done. Get out of my house!"

"What?", I asked in disbelief.

"You got 10 minutes to get your shit and get out. If you're here in 11 minutes, I will shoot you and bury you in the desert with the rest!" He then turned to Roderick. "And you? You're fired. Hit the bricks or you're dead too. There's no room for traitors in my organization."

Roderick returned the gun to his belt, teeth clenched in anger. He stared into Gorman's eyes with fury. "Fine," he snapped. He glanced over to Jolene and me. "Sorry girls, you're on your own now." He spun around and stomped off, leaving me speechless.

Barrington lowered his gun, ordering, "Jolene, go to our room. Lock the door. Let no one in but me." She passed him a tearful glance and scampered away, leaving Barrington, Billy, and me in the driveway.

Darius turned to me, the gun still in his hand. He addressed me, "Jasmine, if you have never listened to me, I need you to do it now. Pack your bag and go to the casino. I will call ahead and make sure they have a room for you. For once in your life, do not disobey me on this. Take the corvette. Get your things. Go now."

I quickly scrambled, following his instructions, crying like a baby as I ran from them.

Only Barrington and Gorman remained in the driveway. They locked eyes in confrontation. Darius hissed, "That girl did everything in her power to save my child. Not once, but twice. I owe Jasmine everything Gorman! You guys are done? Fine, I'm done too. I quit. Consider this my resignation." Darius spun around and left the boss standing alone beside the limo. He spun around in anger, rage filling his soul as thoughts of Jasmine and Trent Winter having sex filled his mind. He punched the window in the limo, shattering the glass and busting open his hand, blood spilling on the ground.

Gorman stumbled into the house blindly. A trail of blood ran down his clenched fist on the floor behind him. Rosita rushed to his side. "Oh, Mr. Gorman, you're hurt", she flooded, "Let me help you."

Billy growled in rage, picking up a nearby vase filled with flowers. He slung the vase at her, and it just missed her face, shattering on the wall behind her. Rosita backed away, screaming in terror at his outburst.

He glared at the shattered vase and flower petals all over the floor. He made his way to the liquor cabinet, pouring a full glass of whiskey, blood from his hand dripping into the glass and mixing with the alcohol. He put the glass to his lips and drank down a big gulp, burning his throat as it went down. "Fuck!", the boss shouted and threw the glass against the wall, pieces flying down around his feet, bloody whiskey running down the wall.

How could everything break down so quickly, in only a matter of minutes, he wondered. The house was eerily silent. Kevin was gone.

Jasmine was gone. Even Darius and Jolene were gone. He picked up the whiskey bottle and began drinking directly from the bottle. From the corner of his eye, he saw Jasmine sprint out the door with a small suitcase. A brief feeling of regret sank into his soul.

He knew he had anger issues and jealousy that needed to be worked out. But he couldn't decide if his regret was over the fact everyone left him or over the fact, he didn't shoot Jasmine in the head when he had the chance to.

His haunted past of his former wife cheating on him ate at his soul. He had invested a year. A year of war, only for Jasmine to turn on him and betray him with the enemy. All to save some unborn kid. He should've ordered Darius to go through with that abortion from the very beginning. And now look… it cost him everything! His entire family was gone. Gone just like that, in a matter of minutes.

CHAPTER 10

The valet took my corvette and handed me the ticket. He neither spoke nor looked me directly in the eye. I dragged my luggage behind me, trudging towards the front desk. I was met halfway by the casino manager. Quickly he sputtered, "Mr. Barrington called me. Follow me, Miss Jasmine. Speak to no one. If you need anything you call my cellphone only. I will see that a decent meal be brought to your room. I am here to serve you. Mr. Barrington will have further instructions for us." He led me to a very nice room on the top floor. "The bar and the snacks are fully loaded for you." Our eyes met and each of us saw the sadness of this situation. He nodded and vanished. I entered the room and put my bag in the corner, sitting on the bed in silence. I could contain my emotions no more and broke down in tears. I had been more welcome in the arms of the enemy than my own true love.

As the RV rolled on through the desolate desert, Aguzzi finally asked Winter about the events on the last day. Sipping from a glass of straight up gin, he asked his boss," So, why didn't you take the girl, boss? Do you like this woman? You could've made her do anything and you chose not to? You realize Gorman may kill her. He was very pissed off."

Trent sighed, "Yes, that's a good possibility. I can't help that. I offered her to join us, and she refused. If she lives, she will come to me in time. I'm a patient man. To the winner of the war goes the spoils," he grinned. "Actually, I couldn't have planned this any better myself, Sal. That woman wrecks me," he added with a sigh. "Let's go home."

Winter took the guitar from the closet and began to play, sitting in a chair. He played a slow, soulful tune. "Boss? Why didn't you? You obviously wanted to."

Trent answered sadly, "I figured the organizations have taken enough from her."

Sal shrugged, not sure what he meant, but decided to leave well enough alone and walked away in silence, pouring another gin. Winter closed his eyes, lost in the tune, and feeling the music take him to another reality.

I stayed in my room at the casino for 3 days without coming out. Barrington said that this might blow over in a few days, but I didn't believe him. I paced the floor. My mind couldn't handle all that had happened. The four walls were closing in and I had to get out of there. On day 4, I decided to take a stroll down to the casino floor.

Entering the floor, I felt all eyes upon me. It was evident that the rumor mill had gotten wind of our breakup. Whispers from the workers penetrated my ears. I ignored them, gossiping and staring at me. I felt like such an outcast, rejected by the boss and nothing more than used goods. Damn, it was just like Winter said it would be. I passed faces of cold stares, shunned. No one spoke to me. Couldn't they see my heartbreak? My humiliation?

I tried hard to be brave, to be strong. Inside, I was torn up. How could I be the villain in this? Gorman had killed my mother, tossed me away because I tried to save a baby. And yet, they looked at me like a traitor.

Gamblers were filling the casino floor as I made my way to the bar and ordered a Pina Colada. The bartender sat it down in front of me, and when I tried to pass him the money for it, he shook his head. "You pay for nothing here, Jasmine. All on the house. Barrington's orders."

I sat down at a nearby table alone, sipping from the delicious frozen cocktail. I sighed, not knowing how anything could be fixed at this point. From across the room, I caught a glimpse of Billy. My heart both leapt for joy and cried out at the same time. I wanted to run to him. I wanted to scream, "you murderer." I wanted to fall into his arms. I was filled with so many thoughts and overwhelmed by emotion. I wanted to run to him and beg him to please just talk to me.

I rose to my feet. My approach was instantly stifled, as I saw the two hookers on his arms. They were laughing and flirting with him as they strolled across the floor towards the elevators to go up to the rooms. He wore a smile, a playboy aura that shined like diamonds with each step. The women hung on his every move, making obvious sexual gestures, and rubbing up against him promiscuously.

As they made their way to the elevators, I found myself moving across the casino in the same direction. I stared straight at them, moving directly across the casino floor towards the elevators, mindlessly. Not even knowing why, but by some strange pull it had on me.

We met at the elevators at the same time in an awkward face to face. I said nothing. He said nothing. But the two women with him were very uncomfortable, squirming and cowering at the tense exchange of stares. His face was expressionless as he gazed into my eyes. The elevator doors opened and the 3 of them went inside to continue on their sexual journey. When the doors closed and they were out of sight, I spun around and closed my eyes, shaking.

A tear rolled down my cheek. I opened my eyes and every person on the casino floor was looking at me. My pain and sorrow were on full display for all to see. Their faces no longer held anger at the traitor, but sadness for the one shattered. All gossip stopped, replaced by disgust at what they had just seen. I couldn't push the sight of Billy and those two women from my mind. It was too much for me to take. I had to get out of there.

I stormed to my room and slammed my belongings into my luggage. I took a steak knife I had left from the previous evening meal and walked into the bathroom, crying profusely. "It's over," I wept. "It's really over." I broke down, sobbing and staring at my reflection in the bathroom mirror. I picked up the steak knife and just started cutting into my shoulder, pulling the tracking device out that Billy had implanted in me to protect me from Trent Winter. What did he care? He was no longer my protector. I was on my own. The bloody tracking device fell into the sink. I took a white towel and soaked up the blood. Tossing the blood-soaked towel on the floor, I stomped back to the bed and picked up my bag. In rage and sadness, I ran from the hotel room blindly. How much could one person take? I ran to the valet and shoved the ticket at him, crying, but not saying a word, as blood dripped down my arm onto the concrete.

He quickly brought the corvette around and held the door open, fear in his eyes. "Miss Jasmine, you're bleeding. Where are you going?"

I tossed the bag into the passenger's seat and ignored his questions. I slammed the door shut and revving the engine, peeled out of the valet parking, leaving smoking tire marks behind me. I drove blindly, as fast as I could without stopping, nearly causing several accidents. I didn't care. I just wanted out of there and the pain to stop.

Gorman sat on the edge of the bed as the two hookers produced several lines on cocaine for them in preparation for their sexual encounter. They took off their skintight dresses and tossed them across the room playfully. In only their thong underwear, they snorted a couple of lines of coke, passing it to Gorman.

Gorman glared straight ahead, unaware they were even nearly naked and dancing around. His eyes did not see them. He only saw Jasmine's face. The pain and tears in her eyes. The hurt he had caused. The two women looked at each other and shrugged, not knowing what to do. One finally asked softly, "Mr. Gorman??"

"Get out," he said flatly. "Go on, take the money and get out."

"Did we do something wrong?", she asked in fear, afraid of what the pimp would do to her in punishment.

"I said get out!", he growled loudly in anger.

The other prostitute picked up the dresses from the floor and they hurriedly put them on. As they took the money and reached the door, she turned back to Gorman and quietly whispered, "If you love, why don't you go after her?" They departed him, as he puffed up in rage and jumped to his feet, ready to destroy anything in sight. As they scampered away in terror, he fell back on the bed and laid down, closing his eyes. He was so tired. "Fuck!" he sneered to himself.

Tears rolled down my face as I drove. I could hear Trent Winter's voice in my head over and over saying that when Gorman was done playing with me, he would either put a bullet in my head or throw me out like yesterday's trash. Las Vegas was in my rear view as the sun was rising. I was driving at more than 120 mph and not even sure of my destination. What would I do now? I was vulnerable to be captured again by Winter, and he might not be so charitable this time.

Billy's eyes opened quickly. Where was he? He glanced around the empty hotel room, trying to clear the sleep from his brain. He sat up slowly on the edge of the bed and glanced to the clock on the side table. He had slept 4 hours. He went to the window and pulled back the curtains, blinded by the sun shining into the room. His heart was heavy in his chest. Jasmine. The disks. The war. Barrington and Jolene. Kevin. The events played out in his mind like a movie. He looked at his reflection in the windowpane. He looked horrible. The stress was taking its toll. He sighed. He knew what he had to do.

Gorman approached the front desk and saw the casino manager in the corner. He made eye contact with him in the distance. "Take me to Jasmine, now.", Billy demanded.

The manager's face went ashen, "She's not here, Mr. Gorman. Take a break everyone, leave the front desk for a moment." All of the desk clerks exited without any hesitation.

"What do you mean, she's not here? Barrington has a room for her here."

"She left without checking out or saying anything to me about three and a half hours ago, sir. Took the corvette and sped out of here like the wind. She had her bags with her. I was hoping she was going home. I guess not."

"Why didn't somebody stop her?" He stood quietly, not knowing how to answer that question. "Where is she going?"

"I asked the valet what she said, Mr. Gorman. He told me that she didn't say anything. She was crying and bleeding."

"Bleeding?"

"Yes, he said blood was dripping down her arm."

Gorman closed his eyes. The tracking device. "Get my car!"

The boss came to a screaming halt at the security gate of his estate. "Is she here?!", he demanded.

"She? Who?"

"Jasmine! Don't play me! Is she here?"

"No, sir. She has not returned."

Gorman stomped on the gas and sped down the long driveway towards his house. He stormed inside, stepping over the broken vase that still remained on the floor from his previous temper tantrum. He went straight to the Barrington wing with purpose. He burst into Darius's private living quarters and made his way into Barrington's bedroom, shoving the bedroom door open with a bang. Barrington jumped to his feet, gun in hand. "What the hell do you want?", Darius shouted.

Billy passed him without even looking at him. He went straight to the bed and ripped the covers off of Jolene, pinning her below him. "Where is she?", he screamed in her face.

Jolene was instantly awake. "What? What are you talking about? Where's who?"

"Jasmine! Where is she?", he growled, veins popping in his neck.

"At the casino. You know that. Darius got her a room there and told her to stay there till we figure out where we are going to go. We'll be out of here any day, Gorman. Darius got hired on in California."

"She's gone! She took the corvette and left the casino. I've tried calling her a dozen times and she's not answering her phone."

Barrington spat, "Just use the tracking device and leave us the hell alone, Gorman."

"She cut the fucking tracking device out and left it in the hotel room. Where is she?!"

"What?! Why would she do that? She would never do that! She knows that Winter can find her!"

"Call her, Jolene. You call her. She'll answer for you. Right now!"

Fumbling nervously as Barrington looked on, she grabbed the phone off of the nightstand and started dialing, Gorman still straddling her body in the bed. The phone just rang and rang.

"She's not answering me, Billy. That's not like her. She always answers my call. What's going on?"

Barrington snorted, "Well, you totally screwed the pooch on this one, didn't you Gorman?" Jolene's mouth flopped open. Was Darius really talking back to the boss like this? Wait, Gorman was no longer his boss. Wow, the realization shocked her.

"We need to find her. She has the disks!", Billy hissed, getting off of Jolene's body and walking towards the door.

Barrington sighed. "She took the disks. Shit, that's not good. She's not safe now."

"She never was," Jolene protested in anger. "Winter wants her you guys. Damn it!"

"Call her!", Gorman insisted.

"I just did! She's not answering me either, Billy. What are we going to do? She's on the run."

"I told her to stay put!", Darius added sharply. "Why would she suddenly break and run now, after 3 damn days?"

A wave of guilt washed over Gorman. He knew why she ran. She ran because of the hookers. He hadn't even slept with them, but deep inside, he knew this is why she ran. Billy ordered, "Get dressed, you have to find her!"

I had been driving and crying for a long time. The road flying under me at over 100 mph for hours. Road signs read Albuquerque, NM. I was tired of these damn disks. I glanced at the bag in the passenger's seat. Maybe I should destroy them. Burn them in a bonfire. They contained nothing but pain and sorrow. Tired of the war. Tired of waiting for Gorman to ever love me. Tired of all the screaming and fighting. My soul was weary. My eyes were weary. I was just so damn tired.........

I opened my eyes with a gasp, pain surging through my whole body. What the hell? Where was I? What was this shit all over me? I grabbed the face mask in an attempt to rip it off of me.

"Don't do that, Ma'am," a strange voice said calmly. "You've been in a bad car accident. Your car went off of the road and rolled over several times. You're injured. I need you to stay still. We're transporting you to the hospital right now."

"Where's my bag?", I gasped between pain shockwaves. The pain killers and sedatives started kicking in.

"Your bag is still in the vehicle on the way to the impound lot. You can get it later. The lot is a secure location, and it will be safe."

"My arm," I groaned.

"Your arm is broken, Ma'am. You have a concussion, major lacerations, and internal bleeding. It was a bad accident."

"Fu...." Darkness overtook me. I briefly woke up in the emergency room with several doctors and nurses hovering over me. I groaned in pain and ripped the oxygen mask off, thinking it could be sleeping gas like Winter used at the casino. There were IV's and machines hooked up to me. I started thrashing about, "No, I have to get out of here," I mumbled.

"Ma'am, you shouldn't move," a nurse instructed. "We'll give you something for the pain."

"No, you don't understand – Winter."

"Ma'am, that's the concussion. It's spring, not Winter. It's May. You're confused. Just relax now. We have to set this arm."

"No. I have to get out of….." Darkness once more.

When I finally woke up again, I was in a private room. My arm was in a cast. Several bandages covered lacerations, including where I had cut the tracking device out of me in the hotel room.

A nurse happened to walk in. "Ah, good, you're awake," she smiled. "How are you feeling? You've been asleep for 2 days. You're lucky to be alive."

"Are my clothes here?"

"Yes, ma'am. Why?"

"My cellphone is in my jeans pocket. Can you get that for me?"

"Yes, of course." I watched as she picked the blood-soaked jeans up and riffled through the pockets, pulling out my phone. "Now that you are awake, we can finally get some personal information. We have you listed as a Jane Doe. I am curious about these old wounds you have on your back and what happened there. It almost looks like whip marks, isn't that crazy?", she laughed. "Ring the bell if you need anything."

She breezed out of the room. I moaned softly, feeling horrible. Everything hurt. The corvette was in impound. The damn disks were in the car. I had to get to them before anyone else. Where was I? Albuquerque. Whose territory was this? Was I in Winter's territory? And now they were asking questions about the whip marks. What was I going to do? I had no one to turn to. The cellphone in my hand, I openly wept.

I turned the phone on. 38 missed calls from Jolene. I dialed the only person on the planet I could trust, and between the sobs I pleaded, "This is Jasmine. I need your help. I'm alone and scared. I'm hurt. I have to get the disks back, I lost them. I'm begging you to please help me. Please. I have no one else I can turn to. Please."

CHAPTER 11

Billy Gorman stormed around the house. He swept up the broken vase. There was no Rosita. No coffee. No breakfast. His stomach rumbled from too much whiskey the night before and no food. Making his way into the kitchen, he caught a glimpse of Rosita's husband, who did the gardening and landscaping. He was at the kitchen sink getting a glass of water. "Where the hell is Rosita?", he questioned sternly.

"I'm sorry, Mr. Gorman, but she is too afraid to come into the house. She will not leave our room."

Billy could see his temper had gotten way out of control and had driven everyone away. "Ok. Whatever," he mumbled. He rummaged through the pantry and came up with the only thing he knew how to make- a peanut butter and jelly sandwich.

Jasmine had been gone almost 3 days now and Billy realized that she wasn't coming back. He hadn't slept. Hadn't eaten. Hadn't showered or shaved. He hadn't even gone to the casino. He plopped down in the kitchen chair and took a bite of his PB &J. Memories of everyone gathered around this table in laughter haunted his mind. For the first time in his life, the boss felt very alone. How had everything gone so wrong?

His phone went off in his pocket and he answered it sadly. "Gorman."

It was the front gate. "Mr. Gorman, that US Marshall is here, and he is insisting he speak with Jolene. He says it's urgent."

"Could that asshole pick a better time to torment me?" Billy moaned, "Damn it. Go ahead and let him in. We'll meet him at the front door. Call Darius and have him bring Jolene."

It was an awkward moment when Darius, Jolene, and Billy all met at the front door. They weren't exactly on good terms. They had barely spoken and had managed to avoid each other. He saw them bringing in boxes to pack their belongings and he wanted to stop them, but at this point he didn't know how.

When the doorbell rang, Barrington opened the door. Joseph Landry stood before them, an odd look on his face. "I need to talk to Jolene alone", he said softly.

Barrington abruptly replied, "Whatever you have to say to my wife, you can say in front of me."

Landry squirmed, eyes locking on Jolene's. She sighed, "Now's really not a good time, Joseph."

"Spit it out. What do you want?", Darius growled. "What's so damn important?"

Landry stepped side to side, looking around them into the house, as if looking for somebody. "Jasmine." Everybody standing at the door stiffened, the hair standing up on the back of their necks.

"What about her?", Gorman demanded coldly.

"Jolene, are you sure you wouldn't rather us speak in private?"

Barrington puffed up, standing close to her in protection mode. "No. It's ok, Joseph. Go ahead. What is it?"

"Is she here?"

"What do you want?", Gorman repeated with aggravation.

"She's not here, is she?" There was a long pause. "I got a phone call from the Chief of Police in Albuquerque this morning. He is a good friend of mine."

"Congratulations," Barrington snarled, "Thank you. Have a good day." He tried to close the door, but Landry stuck out his foot, blocking the door from closing.

"A Jane Doe with whip marks on her back turned up in their hospital. The description matches Jasmine. Somebody want to tell me what is going on?"

In a hushed tone, Jolene asked, "You said hospital. Is she…"

Joseph took her hand, much to the displeasure of Darius. "No, she's not dead. She was in a very bad car accident. The corvette went off the road and rolled over several times. She is hurt quite badly. Anyone here have the balls to tell me how this happened?" Landry was staring Gorman down in a challenge. Gorman shifted his weight confrontationally.

Jolene was at her breaking point. She spoke up, "Enough of this macho bullshit guys. My sister is hurt and needs me. You two dickheads want to fight it out, go for it, but I'm going to go get my sister whether ANY of you like it or not. Get the fuck out of my way." She took a couple of steps toward the garage to confiscate a vehicle.

Landry grinned, "Well, I guess she told you. She's cranky now that she's pregnant, isn't she?"

"You have no idea," Barrington whispered, following after her.

Gorman brushed past Landry, shouting, "Wait, we'll take my private plane."

In seconds, they were gone, leaving Joseph standing alone in the doorway. "Damn it," he snarled, "Nobody told me what the fuck is going on."

Billy called ahead on the way to the airport, and they had his jet fueled and ready to go upon their arrival. They quickly boarded and strapped in. There was no reason to be nice anymore, and Barrington said, "Why the hell are you going? What do you even care? Oh yeah, you want the disks. You do know that those officially belong to Jasmine, not you, right?"

Gorman glared at Barrington but did not reply to his snarky tone. Jolene elbowed her husband to shut up. After all, Gorman was kind enough to let them use his jet. Darius closed his eyes and pretended to go to sleep, so to not have to interact with Billy.

The boss tipped his head and looked eye to eye with Jolene. She did not flinch or allow him to intimidate her. "You're very pushy now that you are pregnant," he mocked.

Her response shut him down and made him go silent. "We are all family here, Billy. We are ALL we have. Yes, I'm passionate about finding my sister. I just wish we could act more like a family and less like just business associates, but I guess that will never happen until we all learn to appreciate each other and what we have."

Darius smiled. He kept his eyes closed as if he was still sleeping. "Passionately pushy."

Billy smirked and sat back in his seat as the plane taxied down the runway. But something about what she said to him stuck in his mind. They were family.

Upon entering the hospital in Albuquerque, Jolene sprinted to the front desk and out of breath, demanded, "I need to see my sister!"

"Name?"

"Ja…", Barrington stepped on her toe to shut her up. "Well, I believe they have her under Jane Doe. She was in a very bad car accident. A corvette. Dark hair."

The nurse narrowed her eyes at the group, suspiciously interrogating, "The one with the whip marks on her back?"

"Room number," Gorman said coldly.

"Funny thing", the nurse said with a grimace, "she asked for her cellphone and made a call. A short time later, a tall man in a fedora and trench coat came and whisked her away. I went to check on her and she was gone. The IV was pulled out and all of the machines were turned off. Nothing in the bed but blood stains. So, I want to know who this woman is."

"Gone? Are you sure? Do you have video of who took her?"

"No. That camera has been broken for 2 months."

Billy's mind was whirling. Trench coat. Winter had been known to wear a trench coat in the past. She called the enemy? Why would she call the enemy? "Winter," the boss sighed.

The nurse rolled her eyes. "That's what she kept saying. Don't any of you people know it's May? It's spring, not winter!" She started to walk away and then stopped, "You know, we need some answers from you."

Darius said calmly, "You want answers? Go ask the frigging Chief of Police." She was flabbergasted by his rudeness. "Come on, let's go. We're done here."

Once the trio was sitting back in the plane, Jolene asked, "Billy, what makes you think it was Winter that took Jasmine?" She was quiet for a moment. "I have a plan."

"You have a plan. The pregnant and passionate one has a plan. So, please do tell."

"Don't patronize me asshole!" she shouted at him.

Barrington smirked at Billy, with little faith in his wife. "So, darling, what's your plan?"

I sat in the front passenger seat of a Dodge Charger, groaning in pain. "Thank you."

He said, "You have internal injuries and a concussion. You should be in a hospital."

"No. I can't. I can't take a chance. You know they are loyal to Winter here."

"You need to tell me what happened in that RV between you two, Jasmine, because the woman that came out isn't the same one that went in."

"We have to get to the impound, so I can get the disks from the corvette. Can we just go and talk about this later?"

"You're the death of me, girl."

"Why does everyone say that?"

We pulled up to the gate house of the impound lot. My driver rolled his window down and said, "Hey we need to get some papers out of our car that was in an accident a couple of days ago.'

"No can do, buddy, we're closed. You gotta come back Monday morning."

"That's two days from now."

"Oh, you figured that out all on your own genius? Right! It's Friday night. Come back Monday."

The driver turned to me. "I tried to be reasonable with him." He reached in his jacket and pulled out a 9mm handgun and shot the single gate guard in the chest and head 3 times, killing him. He got out of the car and pushed the button, opening the gate.

When I saw the corvette, I gasped. It was all smashed up. How did I possibly survive that? I reached through the broken-out windshield and grabbed up the bag that had the disks in it. I heard sirens in the distance. "Gotta go, Gotta go," he shouted from the running vehicle. I jumped into the car, and we sped out of the impound lot and down the road, as the police were coming into sight. I breathed a sigh of relief. I had the disks back in my possession once more. I was safe and had my disks. Thanks to him.

On the plane, Darius and Billy humored Jolene by listening to her plan to rescue Jasmine from Trent Winter. Barrington chuckled, "Jolene, that's bold. It's crazy."

Gorman stroked his moustache, intrigued. "That might just be crazy enough to work."

"With just the 3 of us?", Darius argued. "Do you know how risky and ballsey this is?"

Gorman grinned, "That's why I like it. They'll never see it coming."

Barrington shook his head side to side. "You two are nuts. Totally crazy."

Billy and Jolene gave each other a high five, chuckling. Darius moaned, "Damn it, Jasmine, you're going to be the death of us all. I'll tell the pilot. It's New York City. But for the record, I do not like this idea at all."

I gripped the door handle of the Charger. "We can slow down now. I don't want to be in another accident." He dropped the speed, knowing the police were not in pursuit.

"So, where are we going, Jasmine? It's just you and me now. What's our destination? You know you should be in a hospital."

"Don't start that again, please. No hospitals. They aren't safe from Winter."

"So where is it safe?"

"Someplace far away."

"And where's that?"

"Home," I said fondly. "We're going home."

CHAPTER 12

"This is it. This is the place," Barrington spoke out.

"Are you sure?", Billy inquired nervously.

"Yeah, I'm sure. I had pictures from someone on the inside."

Jolene whispered, "I'm scared."

"Yeah," Barrington snickered, "We all are honey. Just do your part and leave the rest to us."

"It worked at the house for Billy," Jolene added quietly. "Element of surprise. This will work. Why can't it work here?"

Darius grinned, "Uhh…. armed guards for one."

"Yeah, there is that."

Billy whispered cautiously, "What if she doesn't want to come back with us?"

"Why the hell wouldn't she want to come back with us?", Jolene blurted out, not knowing about Gorman and the hookers.

"One problem at a time," Darius instructed, pulling a ski mask down over his face. Billy did the same, stepping from the vehicle.

The New York City Street was fast asleep. It was 3AM in a rural upscale Manhattan suburb. "I don't know if this looks real. I mean ketchup, really? I need one of you guys to hit me," she said.

"I'll do it," Gorman volunteered.

"No. Nobody hits my wife."

Gorman smiled, shrugging. Jolene squirted ketchup down the front of her and tore her shirt, tousling her hair. She stumbled up to the door and pounded on the glass. Two men approached the glass doors but did not open up. They were obvious guards. Jolene pleaded through the glass doors at the men, "Please help me. I was just mugged. They got my purse. I have to call the police. Quickly, I want them to catch the mugger. Help me, please. I think he's still out here lurking around!" She poured on the tears, limping. She dabbed her palm into the ketchup and placed a "bloody" handprint onto the glass door, dragging it down in a smearing motion for effect. Her make up job of bruising was very convincing. They hesitated.

"Get out of here, lady. You got the wrong address! You can't come in here. Beat it! There is a gas station 2 blocks down. Go there!" They unlocked the door and opened it, pointing a gun at her. Jolene collapsed in the doorway, as if fainting, blocking the door open. She twitched a couple of times as if she was having a seizure, then went totally limp as if she was unconscious. She sold it like a professional.

"What the fuck", the guard sputtered, "Get this broad out of here."

As he reached down to drag her limp body out of the doorway, Gorman and Barrington, in their ski masks rushed them. Taser stun guns at max, they let the 2 guards have it with a huge charge. The guards dropped their guns and fell to the floor, twitching uncontrollably like a fish out of water and foaming at the mouth.

"We're in", Barrington said, dragging the bodies behind the front desk of the hi-rise. "Elevator, 15th floor," Darius yelled. "We don't have a lot of time here guys. Jolene, get back to the car!"

"Hell no, Darius. This was my idea. I'm going with you. That's my sister, damn it!"

He groaned. There was no time to argue. They stepped into the elevator and both Billy and Darius took the automatic weapons in hand. As the elevator ascended, Darius chuckled, "Well that worked out better than I thought it would."

"On point, we're not there yet", Gorman instructed. The elevator came to rest on the 15th floor and the doors opened. This was the enemy's layer. Trent owned the entire floor, and his domicile was not difficult to spot.

Darius warned, "This isn't going to be quiet," as he pulled a very small amount of C4 from his bag. "We'll have company fast."

Gorman nodded, "Do it."

Under a controlled and muffled sound, the C4 blasted the door wide open. Flashlights and machine guns in hand, they stormed the flat like a well-trained swat team. They quickly knew the way to Winter's bedroom and sprinted there, placing the machine gun against his forehead as he slept.

With force, Gorman shoved the barrel of the gun into his forehead. "Wakey, wakey mother fucker."

Winter sprang alive as both guns were now on him in his bed. "Watch the door," Barrington shouted to Jolene, who also had a gun, but terrified if she had to actually pull the trigger.

Trent snarled, "Barrington? What the fuck do you want? Invading my home like this."

Jolene turned on a light switch, light flooding into the room. "Where's my men?", Winter demanded. Gorman pushed the barrel harder into his forehead.

"Turnabout is fair play for the casino, asshole", Gorman snarled viciously.

Trent Winter suddenly came fully awake and observed the gravity of the situation. "Just you 3?" He laughed. "A little under manned if you will. And now Barrington has turned his pregnant wife into a gun moll? Well, isn't this just too precious?" He seemed quite amused.

"Time's ticking," Jolene shouted from the door, where she stood guard in fear.

Winter put his hands in the air, still snickering over the ridiculousness of the effort. Gorman glanced at his headboard and saw a photo of Jasmine at his bedside. Enraged, he growled, "Where is she?"

"Where is who?", Winter responded, growing weary of the game. "Can I get out of this bed? I have no idea what the hell you are talking about." He slowly rose from the prone position to his feet.

"You took her, you bastard, and we want her back. You took her from the fucking hospital, and she is bleeding internally."

Winter stood in his boxing shorts, arms up in the middle of his bedroom. "What the bloody hell are you rambling on about? Have you lost your fucking mind?"

"Jasmine," Gorman shouted. "Where is she?"

Winter responded, "Take off those ridiculous masks, and look me eye to eye, man to man." Without hesitation, both Gorman and Barrington took off the masks to face him down.

"Now let me get this straight. You've lost Jasmine, and you think she is here with me?"

"Where is she?", Jolene demanded from the kitchen. Winter caught her staring at him in his boxers and gave her a pelvic thrust in her direction. She sneered, "Somebody shoot his dick off."

Winter smirked at Jolene, "Love, if I had Jasmine, she would've been in that bed beside me."

Jolene glanced at her watch. "We need to know where she is right now!"

"Pushy, isn't she?"

"Passionate," Barrington corrected.

"Well, as you gentlemen can see, I don't have her." Winter's eyes gleamed, "So Jolene going to be your strong arm in California?" He revealed he knew about the breakup of the organization with arrogant glee.

Leaving her post, Jolene stormed across the flat. "Tell me where the fuck my sister is, or I swear to God, you will be my first ever kill!"

Trent saw desperation in Jolene's eyes. He glared at her, slowly answering, "The last time I knew she was at Gorman's casino, and then poof, she was gone. I hope she was headed here, but I do not have her, yet."

Jolene suddenly had the air sucked out of her lungs, for she believed him. The look in Trent's eyes told her he was shocked by the development. "Swear to me," Jolene pleaded, tears in her eyes. "She wasn't the same after you took her last time."

"I DON'T have her, Jolene."

Barrington sighed, "We have to go. We're out of time. We're not going to get any answers here."

"Oh, yes we are", Gorman snarled. "I want to know what happened in that RV! I want to know what you did to her. Did you torcher and rape her? Did she just give herself to you?"

Trent took a step back, puzzled. "Did she tell you I raped her?"

"She hasn't spoken a word to me since she got back. I want to know what you did to her!"

Winter raised his eyebrows at him. "What I did?" He rolled this over in his brain. "I told her the truth, Gorman." He thought about the hit list and what Jasmine had discovered. Cocking his head to one side, he chuckled, "She didn't tell you? She didn't tell you anything?"

"Just shoot him," Jolene cried. "We have to leave now!"

Trent lowered his hands. "You two outside. Gorman and I have to have a conversation. You want to know what happened in that RV? I'll tell you. I'll tell you everything."

"Outside," Billy ordered. "Wait for me. I'll be right there."

Darius protested, "I don't think that's a good idea, Gorman."

"Outside!", he shouted.

Darius and Jolene stepped out into the hallway in silence, waiting for the boss.

"You think I raped her," Trent said flatly. "Well, I didn't, I gave her a pass, Gorman. Why? Because I decided that I want her for myself. I told her that when you were done with her, you would either throw her away like trash or put a bullet in her head. I had no idea it would be so soon. I'll take your leftovers. She accessed the disk Gorman. And you know what she found? Hit lists. Names. Shooters. Paying customers. Dates. And guess what? All of our names were on it, including yours."

Gorman stiffened, squaring his shoulders tensely, hostility boiling up in him.

"That's right," Winter continued in a sneer. "Your name. Her mother's mark. She knows now, mother fucker. She knows. No wonder she skipped town."

The revelation hit Gorman like a sucker punch to the heart. They stood face to face in hatred. Silent. The boss lowered his firearm to his side.

"Gotta go", Barrington called into the flat with urgency. The sound of gunfire echoed, as Gorman turned to fire his way out of the battle.

The road flew by in the Dodge. We rode in silence for hours. I whimpered in pain. Not so much from the accident, but the sight of Billy Gorman with another woman. Two of them to be exact. "Which road?", he interrogated. "Jasmine, which road?"

"East. Go east!"

The shoot out at Winter's had been catastrophic. There was a sea of dead bodies in the high rise. Darius, Billy, and Jolene had made it safely back to the private jet, but not unscathed. Jolene gasped "Darius, you're bleeding!"

He had been shot in the shoulder and leg, blood pouring out onto the seat and floor of the plane. "It's just flesh wounds," he calmed her. Billy sat in the seat dazed and staring into space. He had been so sure that Winter had violated Jasmine. He had been sure that he was the one to pull her from the hospital. Everything he believed was wrong. And damn it, now she knew about the hit on her mother and him being the shooter. Who had taken her? Why hadn't she mentioned the fact she knew about her mother? He was stunned and lost.

"What happened in that RV?", Jolene questioned him. "What did Winter say? What did he do to her to make her run from us, Billy?"

Gorman whispered, "We have to find her. We have to find her." He was distant.

"Are you ok?", Barrington questioned, concerned that he may have been shot and in shock.

"No. I'm not ok. Nothing is ok, Darius." The plane taxied and took to flight, headed back to Las Vegas. Gorman muttered, "I thought he had her. I thought Winter had her. She didn't betray me. Who the hell was in the trench coat?"

"Jolene, please try to call her again," Gorman pleaded. She dialed, but there was no answer.

Gorman closed his eyes. "Tend to his wounds," he instructed my sister to care for Barrington's gunshots. "There's a first aid kit in the overhead."

"Jasmine!", a voice called out to me loudly, interrupting my sleep. "I need to get you medical attention."

"Not till we're there," I protested. "NO. Not till we're home."

"Damn it, you're bleeding internally!"

"I don't care. Just get me home. I don't care if I die there. I just have to go home." He stepped down on the accelerator, as they sped down the highway.

"Jasmine! Jasmine!", he screamed. "We're here. I am in the middle of fucking nowhere. All I see is Goddamn woods. Tell me where I need to go. I need directions, we're not even on the map here!"

I laughed out loud at his panic. "We're here." I rolled the window down and took a deep breath. The fresh fragrance of pine trees and Atlantic Ocean filled my senses. "Home!", I cried. "Home." The road sign read: Freeport, Maine 2 miles.

"Shit!", he snapped. "We're on the edge of the earth. If the world was flat, we would've just fallen off," he complained.

"Stop here", I said, "I need to go into this convenience store for a second." I wasn't long and walked out with beer, jerky, and sandwiches.

Sadness filled me and I sat in the car with tears welling up in the corner of my eyes.

"What's wrong?", he asked.

"They're gone. All of my friends. Everyone who helped me escape Parks. They're dead. Buried in the west cemetery. We're all alone. I thought I could ask for their help. It's just us, Kevin."

He touched my hand. "I promised I would always take care of you, Jasmine. You called, you said you needed me, and I am here. You're not alone. You have me, and I'll kill anyone who tries to hurt you. Now tell me how to get to this God forsaken Stephen King cabin you want to go to. I'm telling you, if I see a killer clown, we're fucking out of here." I gave a half-hearted laugh. Inside, I was devastated. My plans were to utilize the help of some of the locals. Kevin was my only friend. But if Trent Winter came, I knew he could not hold off his entourage all by himself. He hated the woods. Hated wilderness and the animals that lived in the woods. He was a city boy, and yet he came. In my hour of desperation, he ignored his every fear to come to my aid.

We entered the cabin cautiously. It smelled closed up and dusty. Kevin opened a beer, complaining, "Damn it, Jasmine, it is so dark here. If I hear scary music, I'm running." I knew the woods scared him, as he shifted uneasily.

Kevin did a check of the entire cabin to make sure each room was secure. He locked the doors as I thought back to the last time I was here. I was Ken Parks prisoner then. I remembered how he tortured me for the disks. Then my mind turned to Trent Winter. Terrified, I asked Kevin, "What if Winter finds out where we are? I don't think he'll let me go next time."

Kevin pursed his lips, while stuffing jerky in his mouth. He shrugged, nonchalantly and answered, "Then we kill him. We kill them all." I sighed deeply at the prospect. "Now it's time Jasmine. You have to call your sister. You know she must be worried sick about you."

"And say what? I'm no longer part of the organization, Kevin. Am I supposed to tell her? Hate to say this Jolene, but Billy killed my mom so our dad could be with your mom? I don't know what to say to anyone anymore. I'm lost."

He sat his beer down on the coffee table and passed me my phone. "Call her," he insisted. It was really more like an order than a request.

Jolene's phone rang and she quickly picked it up. "Oh my God, Jasmine, are you ok? Where the hell are you? We've been looking everywhere for you. Landry said you were in a car accident. We went to see you and they said somebody came and took you. Billy thought Winter took you, so we went into New York and broke into Trent's house to save you, but he said he didn't have you. Please tell me what's going on. Where are you? Who are you with?"

"I'm ok," was all I could muster to say to her in response to her barrage of questions.

"Jasmine, tell me where you are. I'm coming to get you!"

Holding back tears, I whispered, "Jolene, I can never come back home."

"Jasmine don't say that!! Whatever happened, we can work it out. We're family. I love you."

"I love you too. I have to go now,"

Kevin pulled his side arm. "I have to do a perimeter check, Jasmine. Stay put till I get back. Do they have bears and tigers here?"

"Don't be silly," I grinned, "There are no tigers in Maine." He nodded, exiting the cabin in the darkness. I said softly, "But we do have bears and sometimes a mountain lion."

The door burst open, and Ken Parks stormed inside, snatching me up off the couch by my hair violently. I gasped, a scream billowing out of my lungs.

"Jasmine! Jasmine!" I opened my eyes and saw Kevin standing in front of me. His eyes were wild, as he looked feverishly from side to side. "What is it? What is it?"

My eyes were open wide, heart pounding wildly, as a bead of sweat ran down my face. "Ken Parks is here!"

Kevin softened. "You had another nightmare, Jasmine. Ken Parks is dead." I scanned the room in terror.

"It seemed so real."

"I know. But it was only a dream, Jasmine." I could still feel Park's evil presence in the room. Kevin plopped down on the easy chair next to the couch. He stared across the room. "We're not secure here, Jasmine."

He pulled his cellphone from his pocket and dialed. He tilted his head back and closed his eyes, sighing.

"Who are you calling?", I asked.

He ignored my question and spoke into the phone, "Barrington, it's Kevin. I have Jasmine. We're in Maine at her father's cabin. We're sitting ducks if Winter comes."

My mouth flopped open. What the hell was he doing? What happened to we'll kill them all? Why did he tell Darius? What good was that even going to do? Why was he throwing me under the bus like that?

Gorman sat in the office of his estate, working on the computer. Barrington burst into the door, breathless. "I need a crew. I need shooters and snipers and I need them now!"

Billy said quietly, "You don't work for me anymore, remember?" He glared blankly at the computer screen.

"Now is not the time, Gorman!"

"So, tell me why you need a crew and even more important, why should I care?"

Darius snarled, "Don't be a dick. I know where Jasmine is and I'm going to get her."

Billy chuckled, sitting back in his chair. "We already tried that once and it didn't go so well."

"She's not with Winter."

The boss sat up straight in the chair at full attention. "What do you mean?"

"She finally called Jolene. She's safe for now. But I need to get to her before Winter does."

"Our friend in the trench coat?", he interrogated in a hush.

Darius grinned, "Kevin. She called Kevin, Billy. NOT Winter."

Gorman slowly rose to his feet. "I'll gather the crew. We'll use the jet."

"I have to tell Jolene! She's in Maine."

As Barrington bounded out the door, Billy rubbed his face. He smiled, talking to himself out loud. "She called Kevin. She didn't call Trent Winter."

With one arm in a cast, I was struggling to dust inside the cabin to keep busy. The sun was shining, and it was a beautiful day outside. I opened the door to let the fresh Maine air inside the stuffy cabin. Kevin walked over and slammed it shut behind me. "Jasmine," he scolded, "we are not to advertise "hello, I'm here, come on in and get me". Besides, who knows what kind of hideous woodland creatures could make their way in here."

"But smell how clean and fresh the air is here, Roderick. Oops, I don't know whether to call you Roderick or Kevin anymore."

"Since Gorman fired me, I guess it's Kevin."

"I'm sorry he fired you because of me."

He shrugged, "Don't give me orders and then get bent out of shape when I follow them. Besides, he was being an ass because he thought you betrayed him."

I sighed, "I had to give up the disk, why does nobody understand that?"

"Disk?", Kevin laughed, "he wasn't pissed over the disk. "He was pissed over you sleeping with Winter."

"I never slept with Trent, Kevin. All he did was kiss me. I thought that having only 1 of the 3 disks, we would never get any useful information. I was playing him."

"Playing him? That is a dangerous game you don't want to play, Jasmine."

"I had to get Jolene out of that RV somehow."

"He kissed you, huh?"

"Yeah," I grimaced. "He thought he could tell if we would've been good together from one kiss. Ridiculous, right?" I turned away from Kevin to keep him from seeing in my eyes. He was too good at reading people's faces. I pretended to be dusting a nearby shelf. I was uncomfortable.

"And?", Kevin interrogated. "Would you be good together?"

I stopped dusting and look straight ahead, lost in thought, replying, "We'd be dangerous together."

"I know you're angry at Gorman, but don't ever forget what team you're on."

"I didn't feel like he was on my team when he was stepping on that elevator with those two hookers, or when I found out he killed my mother." Silence filled the room.

"I'm doing a perimeter check."

"Nobody knows we're here, Kevin."

Suddenly the front door swung open hard. I smashed the cast against the bookshelf jumping back in terror, cursing in pain. "Honey, I'm home," Jolene's voice thundered. She ran inside and hugged me tightly, as I flinched in pain, but was so happy to see my sister.

Barrington walked up to us. "Darius!", I smiled, "thank you so much for coming to help me!"

"Are you kidding, Jasmine? You saved my child not once, but twice. You're family. I would die for you. But I don't know how long I can stay at this camp. Please tell me there's running water and we don't have to use a hole in the ground in the back yard for a toilet."

I smacked his arm playfully. "Of course not, silly. It's over there." I pointed towards the bathroom and Barrington winked at Kevin lightheartedly. "Jolene will show you to your room. Goodness, what are we going to do? This is only a 2-bedroom cabin."

Kevin spoke up, "I claim the couch. That's mine. We'll make it work."

I turned to close the door as Billy Gorman stepped inside. I took a step back and froze in fear, blurting out, "What the hell are you doing here?"

Jolene rolled her eyes at me. "It's his plane, his men, blah, blah, blah. Macho bullshit. He insisted on coming." I stepped back another step, bumping into Kevin.

Gorman grunted, "I'll advise the shooters in the trees that we're in combat mode. Eat berries and shit."

Kevin followed him out the door, saying, "I will advise them on the lay of the land. I've studied the perimeter." Why was my heart pounding so hard at the sight of Gorman? I was feeling faint and grabbed the couch for support, so I didn't collapse on the floor.

Jolene ran over to help stabilize me. "Kevin said you refused to be admitted to the hospital, Jasmine. That's not good. I know an old doctor here that will make a house call for me, and I know he can keep his mouth shut. Come on, sis, you need rest."

She tucked me into the bed, and I closed my eyes. I opened them back up and saw Jolene sleeping in a chair next to my bed. "Hey, sister," I addressed her.

"Jas, you're finally awake."

"What do you mean?", I yawned.

"Doc came by and gave you a kick butt antibiotic. You've been asleep for 2 days."

"What?", I protested, attempting to sit up. The room started spinning.

"Hold on, Jas. Doc said no sudden movement or strenuous activity. Take your time. I don't need you to fall and hurt yourself worse." I sighed, sitting up slowly and putting my feet over the edge of the bed.

Jolene grinned great big. "Boy you missed it, Jas. Guess what happened?" I shrugged, waiting for the cobwebs to pass. "Darius and I have the other bedroom. Roderick took the couch. The shooters protecting the house are using the car outside. Gorman asked where he was going to stay. Roderick told him to pull up the floor."

"No!", I gasped.

"And guess what? He did. For 2 nights he's been sleeping on the cold, hard floor. No bed, no blankets, no pillow, no nothing."

"What are you guys eating?"

"Delivery pizza every day. Man am I sick of pizza."

I blinked in disbelief. "Wholly crap."

As I exited the bedroom with Jolene, I saw Darius and Kevin playing with a set of rabbit ears attached to the television. Jolene announced, "Hey look who's joining the party?!"

"Feeling better?", they asked, frustrated they could not get a clear television station on the old tv.

Gorman walked up to me from the kitchen. He was so close; I could feel his breath on my face. "You slept a long time."

"I'm surprised you're still here," I said quietly.

"I've told him ten damn times, Jasmine, those disks belong to you and he's not taking them."

"Oh," I muttered, a wash of emotional pain sweeping over me like a tidal wave. I found I was no longer angry, just incredibly sad.

He turned to walk away, then stopped in his tracks and turned back to face us. His eyes narrowed on me. "Do you really think that's why I'm here? Doesn't anybody know that I am not here for the damn disks?" He turned to Darius and Kevin. "Anybody?" All eyes were on him, but nobody said a word. Billy held his arms out and growled, "Oh, you want to see me grovel, is that it? You want a show? Fine!"

Gorman got right in my face. "Jasmine, I'm here to ask you to please find it in your heart to forgive me and come back home to Las Vegas with me." I was shocked. That wasn't what I was expecting to hear. He again turned to the guys, "I'm asking everybody to please forgive me and come back to Vegas. I know I overreacted and was an ass."

"You can say that again," my sister mumbled, and he gave her a cold, icy stare.

"Just like that?", Barrington interjected. "Billy Gorman says I'm sorry and we're all to follow you back to Vegas like some fucking Pied Piper? And for what? You're not going to change. Nothing will change."

Gorman stood up straight, a confused look on his face. He looked to Kevin for assistance, but Kevin merely folded his arms across his chest in silence.

The boss turned back to me. "I love you, Jasmine." His words were heart felt and you could tell it was hard for him to be humble before all of us. "You want to see me beg, is that it?" He suddenly dropped to his knees with a thud on the floor. "Jasmine, I'm begging you to please forgive me and come home."

Darius mocked, "You want us back? You've been ordering us around like slaves for years, and we've put up with it because we're the only family you've got. But nobody is going anywhere unless you give us something to go back to. And just throwing more money in our direction isn't going to work this time."

Billy rose back to his feet. "So, what the hell do you want from me?!"

Kevin answered, "Billy, you should know what each of us want here. If you don't, you can just pack up your men, take your plane, and get the hell out of here."

My mouth flopped open at their insubordination. I was stunned. Billy asked snidely, "You catching flies with that thing?"

Jolene spat, "Sure, that's exactly how you talk to someone to get them to forgive you. Jerk." She rolled her eyes at him, and I thought Gorman was going to lunge at her. He stormed out of the front door, and I put my hand to my forehead.

"What the hell just happened?", I blurted out.

Barrington softened, "I'm sorry, Jasmine, but he was totally out of line in Vegas. If we don't put him in check now, it opens the door for him to continue to treat us all like dirt. I hope you understand."

I nodded yes, tears welling up in my eyes as I stumbled to the kitchen table and sat down.

Jolene grimaced, "We were kind of rough on him, Darius. Jasmine still loves him, you know." Darius and Kevin glanced at me. I wanted to shrink under the table. I looked at Jolene and she sighed, "Come on Jasmine. You can't hide it from me. I know you do."

"It's more complicated now," Kevin announced. I had told Kevin about the hit list and seeing Billy with the 2 hookers.

Jolene whined, "Why does everyone know what's going on here but me?"

Billy stomped about on the grass outside, pacing. He had to cool off. Had to pull himself together. He couldn't afford another meltdown. What did they fucking want of him?

One of the guards stuck his head inside the cabin door. "Mr. Barrington, my men want to know where they can sleep now?"

"What do you mean?", Darius questioned.

The boss just kicked us out of the car and drove out of here like a bat out of hell, burning rubber the whole way. Is he coming back?"

Barrington dropped his head, sighing, "I don't know."

Gorman sped down the road, cursing under his breath. He ranted, "Fuck this shit! I sleep on the cold, hard floor, fund this whole expedition, get talked to like some pestilent child. No fucking way. I treat them like slaves?! Bullshit! I pay them all damn good money. They're the only family I have," he raved, driving towards the highway to leave. He went silent. His eyes softened, the rage passing. He took his foot off of the gas pedal and pulled off of the road into the grass. He gripped the steering wheel tightly in his hand, repeating, "They're the only family I have." He sat immobile for several long minutes, the engine idling. "Damn it. Fuck. Shit," he hissed. He pulled back onto the road and made a U-turn.

Jolene rummaged through the cabinets for food. "There's pizza in there," Darius offered as he continued to mess with the rabbit ears to get a station on the television to come in. "There's no stinking signal here," he complained, "because we're in the middle of east bumfuck!"

"Wait!", Roderick offered. "I think I see something. Yes, I'm getting a picture! It's Lawrence Welk and they're doing a polka."

"Noooo....." Barrington lamented.

CHAPTER 13

It was late afternoon. Billy had not returned. I was secretly devastated as I sat at the kitchen table alone. The protection team was laid out across the floor resting. Darius and Jolene were taking a nap. Roderick was outside with the other team on duty.

Suddenly we heard a vehicle approaching. In seconds, the house was on their feet and ready for war. Darius and the men had weapons drawn and ready for action if the enemy got beyond our outside detail. Jolene stood back in the doorway of the bedroom and looked on in fear.

The front door opened with an evil creaking sound, yet not one shot had been fired by our crew or Roderick. Billy fumbled his way inside and went totally still. A smile curled his lips. "Good job," he commented, seeing all of the guns pointed at him. "Somebody want to help me with all of this stuff?" He had his arms full of shopping bags.

"Where have you been?", Darius grilled.

"We can't stay here without supplies. I will be damned if I am eating pizza for the fourth day in a row." He sat the bags on the floor and winked at Jolene who approached him in curiosity. "I have coffee and beer, huge steaks, and even ice cream and pickles. You should bring it in before it melts."

Jolene asked, "You got that for me?"

"I don't know anybody else here who wants to eat that combination but you."

"Did you really do that for me?", she asked softly.

Gorman leaned in towards her. "Your ice cream is melting, baby, go get it."

Jolene bounced out the door, Barrington right behind her. Kevin came in the house and said, "We didn't think you were coming back. Where the hell have you been?"

Billy grinned, "LL Bean. If I have to sleep on the floor, I need a blow-up mattress and sleeping bag. That store is awesome. I spent a couple of hours in there, just looking around."

"You came back," I whispered. "I thought you went back to Vegas."

Barrington charged through the door with several bags. "You should see the size of these steaks and there's fresh lobster!"

Billy walked across the room to where I stood watching the whole development. "I love you, Jasmine. If that means I give up the organization, the casino, everything – I will. I don't want to leave here without you."

"Who's cooking steaks?", Kevin asked, hungry.

"I will," Billy replied, winking at me. "I'm pretty good on the grill. I bet you didn't know that about me."

Jolene smirked, "Can I have ice cream and pickles now?"

Barrington groaned, "Being pregnant is gross."

My sister quizzed Darius in a hushed voice, "Is the band back together?"

"Not yet. The band still has issues to work out."

"Oh," she sighed in disappointment. Jolene and I stared at each other in silence, and she hurried to get her ice cream.

Gorman said nothing, just started unpacking things. "You went grocery shopping?" I asked in shock. The thought of it brought a smirk to my face.

Billy fired up the grill. He had brought a feast back with him. Enough for everyone, including all of the security details. He was indeed a great grill master, and everything was delicious.

I carried out a round of steaks and brought Gorman a beer. As I spun around to leave, he spoke up, "Jasmine." I turned to face him. "I've been trying to talk to you since I got here, but every time we're together, the others herd you away from me. Can I please talk to you now that we have a minute alone together?"

I trudged up to him, not sure what to expect. Was he going to kiss me or stick my head in the hot coals?

"I know you think I slept with those two women, but I didn't, Jasmine. I couldn't take the look of sadness and betrayal on your face. I got up to that room, and all I could see was you. The hurt in your eyes. I sent them away and never touched them, Jas. I need you to believe me on that. I was tired. I fell asleep in the room and when I woke up, I tried to find you to tell you I was sorry. But by that time, you had already left."

"I'll bring us some more corn and potatoes," I said evasively and went back into the house, to let his confession sink into my brain.

With the lack of entertainment, Kevin and Darius decided to build a bonfire in the back yard. We sat in cool evening night. The stars were bright in the night sky. We drank beer and told tall tales of the old days, like cowboys out on the prairie. It was magical.

The medicine the doctor had put me on kicked in and I became sleepy, excusing myself from our cowboy firepit. As I lay down on the bed, I thought about Gorman saying he did not have sex with those women. Love never seemed to be our problem; it was always everything else. I shut my eyes, sighing.

There was a faint sound of the door opening as I drifted off. I smiled; another beer run. The bedroom door burst open, and I sat up like a rocket. Winter held a bloody bullwhip in his fist, sneering "You think I'm done with you? Not by a long shot, Jasmine!" I screamed a blood curdling scream that came from the pit of my gut. I gasped, choaking, and coughing.

Instantly Gorman was by my side, gun drawn and ready to fire. Eyes wide, the room filled with armed bodies, everyone looking at me. I was trembling.

"Sshh," Gorman said tenderly. He sat on the bed next to me, gently calming me. "It was just another bad dream, baby. It's ok. You're safe. We are all here for you. Nobody is in the room. Go, I got this." He holstered the gun and put his arm around me gently. "It's ok baby." He motioned for the crowd to leave us alone, and they all walked out of the bedroom.

Kevin whispered to Darius, "This is happening more and more. The longer we stay in this house, the worse it becomes. Everything here reminds her of Parks and Winter."

"I know," Darius agreed quietly.

I fell into Gorman's arms and wept.

It was so wonderful to have coffee in the morning. We had been without it for days. All of us around the kitchen table was almost like the old days. Kevin went outside to get a briefing from those who kept guard overnight.

The boss gazed at me and said, "Jasmine, let's go take a walk to the ocean. It's just down the hill. I see there's already a path, where you have walked down there."

"Go ahead," Jolene encouraged. "Darius and I will catch up in a minute."

Snagging a jacket and my coffee, I made my way to the door, and we walked slowly down the wooded path to the water's edge. We stared at the water for a few minutes, enjoying the sunrise. Gorman spoke, "We need to talk about the disks, Jasmine."

I lowered my coffee cup, saying defensively, "They belong to me, Billy. I am not turning them over to you or anyone else. Not you, not Winter, and not Landry."

He snared my arm forcefully, nearly making me spill my coffee. His tone was low and cold. He stepped in close to me, inches from my face. "I'm talking about what you discovered on the disk inside Winter's RV."

"So, Kevin told you, huh?"

"Kevin? No. Trent Winter told me everything that happened in that RV."

"Oh, you mean the part where you killed my mother," I said tearfully.

He gave a deep sigh, and looked all about to make sure we were alone. "I need you to know the truth, Jasmine."

"I know the truth. You forced her car into the tree to make the hit look like an accident."

"I understand your anger, Jasmine. But what truly happened is much more complicated than that. And the truth is not to see the light of day except between us – ever."

I snarled, "Why should I listen to anything you have to say to me about that, Gorman?"

His eyes narrowed and he clenched his teeth, "Because I didn't kill her."

"So, the disks lie, is that what you're saying?" My rage was beginning to boil up in me.

"Baby, I need to tell you how it happened."

"Save me the blood and gore," I hissed.

I ripped my arm away from his grip, taking a step back in terror. I sipped from the coffee cup, staring at him over the rim in disgust.

Billy lowered his voice, "Baby, I'm about to tell you the biggest secret of my life. The least you can do is listen."

I put my hand on my hip. "Sure, let the lies flow," I snorted in fury. "Go ahead."

He explained, "I was up and coming in the business. I needed to get more hits under my belt to climb the ladder. I did tell your father I would do the job for him. I didn't know your mother, and I certainly did not know you at the time. I was waiting for her outside the bar that night."

"She never went to bars," I snapped.

"She was that night. She had just found out that your father was cheating on her with Jolene's mother, and she went to drink that off of her mind. She was upset. I'm in the car with the gun. I saw her come out of the bar's back door. I sighted her in and took the safety off of the gun. I was ready to do the job and make my get away, when I saw this guy following her out of the door. Now I had a damn witness. He was chasing her, cat calls, putting his hands all over her. She slaps him and gets in her car. I could see she was crying and upset over this guy harassing her. She sped off. I decided to follow her and take my shot on the deserted piece of road to your house. She must've seen my headlights and thought it was the guy from the bar chasing her. She started driving fast and swerving all over the road, going from lane to lane. My only guess was that she was drunk. Following her, I pulled up to pass and leveled the gun at her. She looked directly into my eyes. Suddenly, she slumps over the steering wheel. She smashed into my car and bounces off into the tree."

"So, you didn't shoot her?", I questioned skeptically. "Just scared her to death."

"No, Jasmine. She panicked and she passed out behind the wheel. I was curious why she would pass out, knowing she was not a heavy drinker. I did get out of the car and check for a pulse. There wasn't one. She was dead, Jasmine, before I ever got near her. I went back to the bar and sat in the corner – watching that man who had chased her out of the bar. He was putting drugs in the drinks of all the women in the bar that night hoping for a date rape. I got a hit that night baby, but it wasn't your mother, it was on that jerk in the bar."

"So why is it on the disk?". I questioned suspiciously.

"Everybody saw the damage to my car. They knew I had agreed to take the job. They all assumed I drove her into the tree. I needed the reputation. I needed them to think I did it to climb the ladder. I took the credit and never told anybody about the asshole in the bar."

"Is this supposed to make me feel better?", I asked with bitterness.

"I want you to know the truth, Jasmine."

I turned my attention back to the ocean and closed my eyes. Tears streamed down my face in silence.

"I'm not proud of what I did, but I did not kill your mother."

I couldn't absorb what he was telling me. I didn't know how to feel about this secret revelation. Did it really even matter? The intention had been there, even if he had not pulled the trigger. I exhaled deeply, filled with sorrow.

I turned back to the boss and interrogated, "Winter said you've been watching me my whole life since the death of my mother. Is that true? Was I next on your hit list- for the disks?"

"Winter said that did he?" Gorman tipped his head to one side, a silent smirk on his lips. "Let's just say I checked in on you from time to time, so when your father put out a call for help against Ken Parks trying to take his daughter and make you his – I figured I owed it to you. I couldn't save your mom, but I could save you."

"How did Winter know you watched after me; after my mother's death?"

"We were both at the funeral in the distance. Remember, before the disks, there was no war. We came to power at the same time: Parks in New York, Me in Vegas. We both used your father's brilliant accounting skills. You need to know, Jasmine, you can never ever repeat what I just told you to anyone. I only told you because I love you."

I turned away from him in silence and left him at the water's edge. I just didn't know what to believe anymore. I wasn't just broken in body but broken in spirit as well.

CHAPTER 14

I walked back into the cabin by myself. Jolene strolled over to me and passed me an inquisitive look. "Everything ok, sis? Thought you and Gorman were going for a walk down to the ocean together. Is he being an asshole again?"

I just shook my head no in silence, as suddenly all eyes were on me. "So, what's wrong, Jasmine?", Barrington questioned. Did everybody see it on my face? I had been forbidden to speak of my mother by Gorman.

"I'm ok. Just my arm is hurting a little," I lied.

Billy came into the house and announced, "Meeting."

Jolene yawned, "Can we do it in an hour? I just need to rest a little bit."

"Ok," the boss conceded, "I'm going into town for more supplies. Kevin, can your team spare you? I want you to come with me."

He glanced at Darius, and Barrington nodded, "Go ahead. I have security here. Go check out this store Billy's been talking about. We need supplies. And pick me up a damn jacket, will you? It's freezing here."

Billy and Kevin left to go into town. Darius and Jolene went to the bedroom to rest. I sat on the sofa alone in the quiet. I wished I could go back to when life was simple. Back to when I was innocent.

One of the guards entered the house and glanced about. "Why are you alone, without security, Jasmine?'

"Do you have a second to sit down with me?", I asked sadly.

"Miss Jasmine, you want me to sit with you?" I shook my head, and he sat on the sofa cautiously. He seemed nervous. "How can I help you?"

"Has Billy always been an asshole?" He looked around the room suspiciously, like this was a trick question or a set up. "I mean, was he nice before I came along?"

The man laughed out loud. "Are you kidding me? You tamed the beast, Jasmine. Everybody can see he cares for you."

"Is he honest?"

The guard laughed even louder. "Did he take the last piece of bacon and deny it?"

"No, I'm talking about real stuff – serious stuff."

"He told you something that you do not believe?"

I shrugged. "Maybe."

"Important things – do not doubt him. He doesn't pull punches if it is important. If he told you that you are beautiful today, then you can believe him. We do not see the scars and bruises from the accident. We see your beautiful soul."

I smiled at his compliment, but then asked slyly, "And Trent Winter?"

He stiffened. "Cold. Cruel. A product of Ken Parks grooming. He is a snake – not to be trusted. Never turn your back on him." He patted my hand softly, "You make Mr. Gorman happy. And when he's happy – we are all happy. Understand?" He quickly exited to get back to his post. Did I have it in my heart to believe Billy? Could I trust him again? Could I forgive him? Again, I contemplated throwing the disks into the bonfire.

The boss and Roderick returned with more supplies. Darius and Jolene stepped out of the bedroom and joined us. "Really?", I snickered.

Barrington winked, "Hey, she is already pregnant. You think I'm going to pass up free sex right now?"

"Meeting," Gorman instructed.

We gathered in the living room and sat in a circle, wondering what Billy wanted now. The boss stood, pacing the floor nervously. There was an odd concern on his face, and I knew it had to be a new security threat. Maybe Winter knew we were here. My blood ran cold.

"Yesterday Barrington issued me an ultimatum. A challenge if you will. You said you're not coming back to Vegas with me unless I give you all something to make it worth it." He gazed directly at Barrington. "In other words, go big or we DON'T go home." There was stillness in the room. "You said you're my only family, and that hit home, Darius. I've thought about that, and you are right. You guys know that I'm not good at apologies. I'm sorry I acted unreasonable and blew my cool. I am asking you once more to come back with me. But I didn't come empty handed." He reached into a nearby bag and pulled out 2 bottles of champagne and a stack of red solo cups.

"You want me to go big? Kevin – I'll start with you. I asked you to protect the girls for a long time now. I know you are ready to go back to your role as my 3rd in command. I know you're ready to go back to your bar and that stripper you are secretly seeing on the side."

Kevin's head popped up and he went stiff. "Oh, calm down. Yeah, I know about that. I know everything, Kevin. You can't keep secrets from me. So, here's what I am offering you." There was a long pause, as we all waited to see what Billy had to say. He shifted on his feet and announced, "I'm calling off the war with Winter. We'll sign a peace deal, and I will share the disks with him. Once the war is over, you will no longer need to protect the women." The room went bonkers in protests.

"Hear me out," the boss retorted, "these disks have done nothing but cause us all pain and loss of life. Kevin, you accepted my request to watch the girls and the fact that they are still alive, tells me you have done a fantastic job, but it's time to end this once and for all. We'll share the disks and let the chips fall where they may. Barrington, all of our funds and accounts have been transferred, correct?"

"Yes," he replied in shock.

"Kevin, I was wrong to fire you and I need you back with me. I need you back as my 3rd in command; where you are supposed to be." The shock on everyone's face was evident. "Nobody answers me tonight. Think about it, Kevin." The silence was deafening.

"Darius and Jolene," he addressed, flopping down on the sofa between them. "This is what I have to offer you. We'll pull out of nearly all the illegal operations. I know you worry about the impact of the illegal activities will have on your child. We're going straight. The casino is profitable, and we don't need much of the below board business. This will keep the gaming commission off our asses. You're welcome," he spat, getting back to his feet before they could answer him. Darius and Jolene hugged each other with a big smile on their faces.

The boss looked around the room. "Don't answer now. We will discuss it further in the morning after you have had time to sleep on it." The room was abuzz with frenzied conversation in excitement.

Billy crossed the room to where I sat on the sofa. He stood directly in front of me, and I felt intimidated. "You think I'm done, Jasmine? No. I'm here because of you. Come back with me." He knelt down in front of me and pulled a box from his pocket. "Jasmine, will you marry me?" He opened the box, revealing a gorgeous diamond ring. "Come back and be my wife. Let's do this right. Don't answer me now. Wear the ring tonight. See how it feels. Think about it. I want all of your answers in the morning. I have to get back to Vegas, but I want all of us to go back together as a family."

He slid the ring on my finger gently as I gazed at it blankly. My heart was beating wildly in my chest. I was flabbergasted. Wholly crap, what just happened?

CHAPTER 15

I didn't sleep at all that night. I lay in bed and stared at the ceiling, twirling the ring on my finger. Billy had confided in me some pretty deep stuff. Could I believe him? Were we really now going to call for a truce and share the disks with Winter? Things were spiraling out of control.

Restless, I wandered out to the kitchen to get a glass of water. In the dimly lit cabin, I saw Roderick stretched out on the couch and Gorman on his air mattress on the floor. There was a sound of rustling on the back patio. There was movement and a scraping sound on the door. I dropped my glass on the counter with a thud, and fortunately it did not break. However, the sound had both Roderick and Billy instantly on their feet with a gun in their hand. They too heard the sound. A rustling and heavy, loud footstep. The gentle rattle of the door being tested. They began giving silent hand signals, telling me to get back into the center of the room.

Together they stepped towards the door, guns ready, with no sound at all. The pair got between me and the door. Gorman tipped his head and took a shooting stand, as Roderick put his hand on the doorknob. The boss nodded and Roderick flew the door open. Guns at the ready they peered into the darkness of night, lit only by a milky moonlight. There on the patio was a huge moose, eating one of the plants on the porch. They were face to face. It dragged its hooves and snorted, lowering its massive rack at them defensively.

Roderick yelled in hysterics, "What the hell is that?" He then let out a blood curdling scream like a little girl and ran inside the cabin, locking himself in the bathroom.

Gorman burst out in laughter. "I'm going to close the door before he comes inside. We don't want him trampling around in the house. Did you see the look on Kevin's face? He was white as a ghost?" The boss got so much enjoyment out of the scene; he could not stop laughing. Darius and Jolene bounded out of the bedroom. Barrington had a gun, his hair a mess, ready to kill.

"What was that awful scream, Jasmine? Did you have another nightmare? Billy, that's not nice to laugh at her when she's having nightmares. Who's in the bathroom? I got to go."

I grinned, "Oh, that's Roderick, but I think he'll be a minute – he has to change his pants." Well, that comment got the boss going all over again.

Jolene knocked on the door softly. "Roderick, are you going to be in there long?"

"Is it gone?", he shouted in terror? "It wants to eat me! Don't let it in!"

Barrington put his hand on his hip. "What the hell is going on here, Gorman?" But he could not answer, laughing until he was out of breath.

The bathroom door opened, and Kevin peered out slowly, looking into the room at us all standing around. "Big. So damn big. Demon creature. I hate this camping shit!"

Jolene shoved him out of the bathroom and rushed inside, closing the door behind her.

"It's only a moose, Kevin," I yawned with a grin. "It was just eating the plant on the porch. It wasn't coming after you. You just startled it. Go back to bed."

"I startled IT?", he sneered. "That thing wants to kill me. Can it get in?"

Billy shook his head no. "It's gone, Kevin. Let's all just go back to bed."

In the morning I was sitting at the table flipping through an old fishing magazine and waiting for everybody to wake up. Jolene walked out from the bedroom quietly, gazing at the men fast asleep. She came up to the table and whispered, "Jasmine, we need to talk. Take a walk with me down to the ocean. Come with me."

"Yeah, in a little bit. I'm waiting for the coffee to brew," I said.

Jolene repeated in a stern voice, "We need to take a walk NOW, Jasmine!"

She instantly sent my brain spinning. The last time she did this, she told me she was pregnant. What could it be now? And down by the water again? Why is it that's where everyone wanted to go to spill their secrets to me? We walked slowly to the water's edge and stared out at the ocean for several long minutes. Jolene was shaking and nervous.

"What is it?", I gulped. "What's wrong?" She glanced around to make sure nobody was close enough to hear our conversation.

She moved in close to me. "You'll never believe what I just found buried in the night table drawer, under some old magazines."

I shrugged. "What?"

"Two more disks. They look just like the others. There's not 3, Jasmine, there's 5!" I suddenly went stiff. "What should we do? Tell Billy and Darius?"

I ran my fingers through my hair, pacing. "Are you sure? Could it be anything else? An old movie, a music CD?"

"No. I don't think so."

"Shit!" My pacing picked up speed as I stared at her in fear.

"We have to tell them, Jasmine."

"No," I muttered in sorrow, "There's nothing on those disks but death and destruction."

"Jasmine!!"

"Leave it, Jolene. Leave it in the drawer! Keep it buried there. No more death, sis, no more death. We can never tell a living soul about this, understand? Never."

From the porch Billy, Darius, and Kevin gazed at us intently, coffee in their hands. Billy quizzed, "What do you think that is all about? What's going on between them two?"

"Not sure," Barrington answered, "But I know it can't be good. Looks like an argument to me."

Kevin put his hand on his hip. "Interesting." His eyes narrowed, intrigued.

As we strolled back towards the cabin, we saw all 3 men watching us. They sat the coffee cups down on the small table and folded their arms across their chests, interrogating, "What's going on, girls?" It was very intimidating.

"Nothing," I lied. "Just a morning stroll. It's good for the soul." Jolene took a step back in fear, remaining silent. I snared her wrist and pulling her behind me, we brushed by the men without another word.

"Why do I feel like we have to worry?", Darius questioned out loud.

A few minutes later they joined us in the cabin. Jolene sat at the table tapping her toe, ignoring them in the room. Darius observed, "You look nervous, Jo."

"Nope. I'm fine. Everything is fine," she blurted out, an obvious lie.

"Uh huh," Barrington commented knowingly, eyes locking with Gorman and Kevin.

The men knew they were not going to get any answers from the girls. "So, let's talk about last night," Billy stated.

"That was a huge animal," Roderick flooded.

"About going back to Vegas," the boss corrected.

Darius announced, "Jolene and I talked about it. We will go back with you. If you agree to take some anger management classes. That blow up was ridiculous, Billy."

Gorman pursed his lips in annoyance. "Ok. Anyone else?"

"I'll go back," Kevin added. "Happy to get the hell out of the woods. But, until things stay settled down with Trent Winter, we keep our plans low profile. The girls are still my responsibility until I know that the truce will hold."

Next thing I knew, all eyes were on me. I hesitated. Would I be the only hold out? "Come back with me, Jasmine," Billy pleaded. "I'll do the stupid anger management classes. I know you were only protecting the baby. I know nothing happened between you and Winter now. He told me everything that went on in that RV. He's wrong about me, Jas."

Somehow, I didn't think Trent told him everything. My mind flashed to the kiss, to him saying I would be <u>his</u> after the boss was tired of me. "Jasmine?", Billy said tenderly.

"Ok," I conceded quietly.

"Great," Roderick chuckled, "Lets get out the wilderness and back to civilization. I'll get the men ready."

Barrington grinned, "He really hates the woods, doesn't he?"

Gorman winked at me, "Screamed like a schoolgirl."

Even though I agreed, I couldn't help but feel some hesitance in my mind. Trusting Billy Gorman again was not going to be easy or come overnight. I did believe him about the hookers but was less sure about murdering my mother.

"Ok. Let's pack up. Where's the disks?" Jolene scrunched up her face and rolled her eyes back into her head. Had this all been a ploy to regain control of the disks again? I slumped back in my seat, gritting my teeth.

It wasn't long before we were ready to go back to Las Vegas. Jolene and I jumped into the car with Barrington as Roderick locked up the cabin. He stood at the cabin door with Gorman. The boss whispered to him, "When we're gone, I want this place burned to the ground."

Roderick squared his shoulders at Billy. "No. You just want to make sure Jasmine has no place to go if she ever leaves you again. This is her safety net. I won't do that to her, and neither will you."

"This cabin gives her nightmares. It reminds her of what Ken Parks did to her."

"Bullshit. You're not using that as an excuse, Gorman. She still needs someplace she feels safe."

"You call this safe, Kevin? You guys were sitting ducks until I brought my men here."

"Gorman, you're not taking this away from her."

"What do you care? You hate camping, remember?"

"Yes, I hate this place. But I love those girls. Damn it, Billy, you can't leave her with nothing left to lose. You've got your fucking disks. Now be grateful and let's go get on the plane. The cabin does not get touched."

"You know I am your boss again, right?" There was determination in Kevin's eyes. "Fine, the cabin stays. Let's get back home."

It was a quiet flight back to Las Vegas, as I stared at the engagement ring on my finger. There was an uneasiness in my gut.

CHAPTER 16

Once we settled in at the Gorman estate, we all seemed to scatter and separate. Gorman went to his office. Barrington and Jolene went to their wing. Roderick disappeared to his quarters. The house seemed empty and hollow. I sat in the media room watching some mindless television show on tv.

From behind me a tender, solemn voice called out, "Miss Jasmine is that you? Are you home to stay?" I spun around and standing up saw Rosita timidly facing me. "Is everyone back?" she asked cautiously, looking over her shoulder for Gorman.

"Yes," I sighed. "We're all back."

"Mr. Gorman hurt you bad. Face all bruised, big cut on your forehead. He broke your arm too?" She was observing all my injuries and blaming the boss for it all.

"I was in a car accident," I replied.

She came up and hugged me. "It's ok, baby. You can tell me that if you want to." It was clear she did not believe me.

"Things are going to get better now," I said in a hollow tone.

"Of course, it is," she whispered doubtfully.

Three days later, the boss called Trent Winter to initiate the peace talks. He had Darius, Jolene and me in his private office at the estate with him on the speaker phone. Gorman dialed the phone. "Winter, it's Gorman."

As Trent's voice filled the room, a knot formed in the pit of my stomach. "What do you want?", he sneered.

"Shut up you dick and listen up."

Jolene sighed, "The start of a beautiful friendship." Her sarcastic remark got shot down by both Gorman and Barrington and she sat back in the chair, silent.

"Get to the point," Winter said, "Why are you calling me? I already told you I don't have her."

"I've got Jasmine. I also have the disks. You interested in seeing what's on my disks?"

Trent's tone turned to interest. "What are you talking about?"

"I'm offering you an opportunity to share the disks in return for a cease fire."

"We sit down with all three disks, and both share the information?"

"Yes. You and me."

Winter's voice went cold. "YOU are not the owner of the disks, Gorman. You have no authority to broker any kind of deal with me. Jasmine is the true owner of the disks, and she alone can negotiate a peace agreement with me."

"That's not happening," Billy fired back.

"Jasmine are you in the room?"

Billy gave me a nasty glance. "Yes, I'm here," I answered Trent.

"Pick up the phone, darling." I reluctantly picked up the handset, our conversation going private, much to the dismay of the guys. Gorman was mad as hell, as Darius also showed anger over Winter's approach.

I put the phone to my ear. "Yes, Trent."

"Are we making a cease fire?"

"Yes."

"I'll show you mine and you show me yours?" The sexual undertone clearly evident. I cleared my throat, unable to respond to his comment. "Give me a day to think it over. When you call, I speak only to you." The phone line went dead. I grimaced to a room full of pissed off faces.

Jolene spoke up, "Well, he is right. The disks do belong to Jasmine, not us. Oh, I hate that man." I sat the receiver down in the cradle.

Billy sat back in his chair and cocked his head to one side. "Well, what the hell kind of horse shit is that?", he grumbled.

Barrington glared at me with concern. "Are you capable of handling this negotiation, Jasmine?"

"What choice do I have, Darius?" My palms went sweaty and there was a pounding in my head. I bit my lip. For a brief moment, I wondered if they would find out about disks 4 and 5. I had to bury that thought quick. That information could never see the light of day.

It was two days later when Winter called us back. Jolene rushed up to me and announced, "Winter's on the phone. He wants to talk to you about the truce. The guys are already waiting in the office." I trudged behind my sister, praying I was up to this task.

As I entered the office, Gorman closed the door behind me. I sighed, "Ok. I'm here, Trent."

"We do this my way, Jasmine," he instructed. "Miami. You and me only."

"No, no," Billy spat, "not going down that way, Winter. Me and Barrington are in on this or no deal."

"Then I bring Aguzzi."

"Fine," Billy hissed. "No other players. No guns."

Trent said in a catty voice," I'll be in touch. Wear something sexy."

"I'll be in my speedos," the boss replied in a snide growl. The boss slammed the phone against the wall.

Jolene blatted out, "Does he like you?" I rolled my eyes and quickly walked out of the room. I went directly to the media room and sat down alone. I stared straight ahead at the blank screen. A silent tear ran down my cheek.

Suddenly Roderick was standing in my view. "Gorman wants this to be just you 4. I don't trust Winter, Jasmine, and I can't be there to protect you. This could all go sideways."

I blinked, "I know."

"Billy says no guns."

"I know."

"You and me. We're going to do a concealed carry class. I'll see you have protection."

"They will probably pat us down or metal detectors."

"I have my ways," he grinned, leaving me in silence. I was so nervous.

Alone again in the media room, my cellphone rang. I picked it up curiously. "Hello?", I answered timidly. I instantly knew it must be Winter. "Hello, Trent."

"Miami. Tuesday. 7:00PM. Gorman knows the hotel. I have a private conference room reserved for us. My favorite color is blue. Be nice to me and wear something blue. Tell that maggot Gorman. Any variance and the deal is off." The line went dead. So, the deal was really going to go down. I couldn't contain the smile – he called Billy a maggot.

Peace between the organizations. I didn't think it was possible. Could I actually pull this off? Gorman wasn't happy that I was the one leading the show on this. After all, it was HIS organization at war. Everything was on my shoulders. Could I trust Winter? Could he trust us? So much could go wrong with this. The weight I carried was overwhelming.

Miami was hot that day. 96 and bright blue skies. We went directly to the hotel on South Beach that Trent had told us about. It was very posh, and the guys wanted to go directly to the conference room. This single hotel was a neutral zone. I lingered in the hotel lobby, trying to calm my nerves. I didn't feel ready to face Winter. Something about him scared me. I wanted to present myself as a professional, so I chose a navy-blue pinstriped two-piece pantsuit with a satin white blouse. I felt awkward, like some kind of lawyer going into a big trial.

As we entered the conference room, I saw that Trent had the entire room set up. There were 3 computers, 3 large monitors, blacked out windows, pens and notebooks, pictures of water and glasses on the tables. Winter stood in the center of the room. Not knowing how to proceed, I strolled directly up to Winter and threw out my hand, offering a handshake. He did not take my hand. Instead, he leaned in close and whispered in my ear, "I think we're a little beyond that, Jasmine. I'm glad you wore blue, but that's not sexy."

"I wasn't allowed," I told him with a hushed voice. I was shaking. Suddenly, Gorman was at my side, interrupting our private conversation, his arms folded across his chest furiously.

Boldly, Trent spoke up, "Pity. It would've made things so much more interesting." He was blatantly pushing Gorman's buttons to see if he was going to lose his cool. Trent pulled a permanent marker from his shirt pocket and without warning, snared my cast, writing something feverishly on it.

He pulled back and got to work. "Aguzzi, block the door. Nobody comes in, nobody goes out." He tipped his head in acknowledgement to Jolene and winked at her arrogantly. That spun up both Jolene and Darius. Barrington's face turned so red with rage, I thought he might have a stroke.

"Alright," I announced, "Let's get this over", I said sharply, pulling the disks from the pocket of my blazer. Winter's eyes locked on the disks. I did my best to ignore him, putting the disks into computer 1 and computer 3. He slid disk 2 into the computer. The room took a collective deep breath as images began to appear on the screens.

Gorman snapped, "Ok. Go sit down now, Jasmine." I turned towards Jolene, off to the edge of the room.

Winter popped up in his chair and stomped over to the middle computer, ejecting his disk. His screen went dark, to a room full of F bombs and cursing. To which he calmly ignored the hysteria and gazing at me across the room growling, "Jasmine, I work with you and not him. How many times do I have to tell you that? I'm getting tired of repeating myself."

I cowered before him like a scolded child.

"What the hell are you doing?", Billy sneered.

"I'm out of here. Aguzzi, let's go."

"No," I pleaded, running to stop his exit. "We need this peace agreement, Trent. Please, I'm begging you."

"Jasmine Grant should never beg," he said with a harsh scowl.

Now Jolene scurried across the room and took a stand at our side. "What if we both beg you," she asked.

Winter replied to her, "You're already out of the game, Jolene. Jasmine bought you that ticket."

"Stop!", Barrington yelled. "Billy, sit down and shut up! Jasmine, take over."

Was I now taking orders from Barrington? Was this going to blow up in my face? Trent took a step around me to leave. For the first time, Aguzzi spoke. "Let Jasmine lead. You ALL follow." Everyone was stunned, including his boss. Silence engulfed the room. "Time to do your thing, Missy. Put the disk back in the computer Winter."

Trembling hands, I pulled the disk right out of Trent's shirt pocket, pleading with my eyes for his approval, terrified. "I'm giving you what you want," I whispered. Fire and rage still blazed behind those dark eyes.

"Go," he agreed coldly. As I turned back to Gorman and Barrington standing in the center of the room, their icy stare made my skin crawl. I went directly to the middle computer with Winter right on my heels. I was so shaky; it took 3 tries to get it into the machine.

"Let's just all sit down," I squeaked, voice cracking. "We need to work together."

Billy had never let me view our disks before, so I was very nervous as to what might be on them. I started all the computers and turned the images over to 3 big presentation screens across the room. To my relief, everybody sat down and started observing what was in front of them. Gorman snarled, "If, I may speak, what we're looking at on screen 1 appears to be Grant's money laundering accounts. Wouldn't you agree, Jasmine?", he questioned in a snide and condescending tone.

"Yes," I replied cautiously. I picked up a laser pointer from the table. "As you can see, some of these accounts are coded. In this column are the transaction dollar amounts. The organization responsible for the money is represented on the next disk, also coded."

"Coded?", the boss said with aggravation, spittle flying from his lips like a mad dog.

Barrington asked softly, "Do you know this code, Jasmine?" All eyes were burning through me.

I cleared my throat and smiled, "As a matter of fact, I do." You could hear a pin drop. I will need paper and a pen, so we can apply the code. It may also reoccur down the road."

Jolene yelled out in support, "You go girl! Woman power." She pumped her fist in the air for encouragement. Darius grinned at her silliness. Gorman was not amused. As I was writing down Dad's secret code to help decipher the information, I noticed Billy and Trent were now jotting down things on paper feverishly. I sat my broken arm on the table to rest it, when my vision caught the message Winter had penned on the cast in permanent ink: ***We'd be dangerous together, love***. I knew that when Billy saw it, he would be angry. I pulled several blank sheets of paper from the stack and rested it over the writing, so he did not see it. Winter coughed and I turned to glare at him. He knew exactly what I was doing, and his eyes were filled with playful joy. To him this was a big game, but I was the one who had to live with the consequences. No sound escaping my lips, I mouthed the words, "I'm going to fucking kill you." He sat back in his chair, barely able to contain the laughter.

"Slide me that code," Trent demanded. I began to pass him the paper.

"Hey, hey," Barrington broke in, "No. Code stays solely with the owner of the disks- nobody else, including us." Winter put his hands up in the air and everyone began writing again, as I verbally translated for them.

When we reached the bottom of the screen, I said, "Ok, now let's move on to disk 2."

"Hold it," Winter protested. "Do your secret button thing."

"What secret button?", Darius interrogated.

Trent grinned, "This is why Jasmine leads. Show them."

I gave him the evil eye. "Ok," I sighed. "See this little icon? It looks like it's just a typo, right? It actually leads to a hidden sub screen if you click on it." With the mouse, I clicked on the icon and the sub screen jumped up on the display. A whole new set of financials appeared. Again, they all went back to writing things down, as I decoded each line for them.

"I have to go to the bathroom," Jolene announced. The guys groaned. "Hey, I'm pregnant. You try sitting here all this time with a bowling ball on your bladder." She strolled up to Aguzzi at the door. "Move, please."

"Ok," I conceded, "Let's all take a break." Aguzzi stepped aside with permission from Winter, and I followed my sister to the ladies' room.

Once we were inside alone, Jolene flooded, "This is going really good." I shook my head from side to side in disagreement and held up the cast so she could read what Trent had written on it. "Why? Why, Jasmine?" I shrugged sadly.

Upon returning to the conference room, we started to go over all of the information on disk 2. Winter instructed harshly, "Use the icon." I shot him a dirty look. He knew what was on the hidden sub screen. Barrington and Gorman also prompted me to do so. Reluctantly, I clicked on the icon. The information about who fulfilled the hit list came up on the big screen.

Darius and Billy suddenly stopped writing. Billy looked over his shoulder at me. His eyes told me to be silent about what he had revealed to me in Maine. A smug little smirk came over Winter's face, as he loved to stir up trouble for us.

Suddenly, Jolene jumped to her feet, shouting, "What the hell is this? Is that your mother's name on the hit list, Jasmine? Gorman pulled a hit on your mom?? And my dad was to blame? What the fuck??!!"

"We'll discuss it later," Billy sneered. Trent watched my reaction.

"No, this can't be right," Jolene continued in an outburst. She spun around to Barrington. "Darius, say something!!"

Sal Aguzzi, standing at the door, laughed out loud, "Damn, it's getting good now, huh boys?"

"Ok, that's enough," Trent instructed as I closed my eyes and put my head in my hands. "Move on to the next disk, Jasmine."

"Move on? Move on?", Jolene snapped.

Gorman stood up and approached her, taking her shoulders in the palms of his hands to calm her down. "Jolene, this isn't the place or the time. I need you to sit and be quiet so we can get through this. Please don't defy me. We will talk later.". Her mouth flopped open in protest. Gorman shook his head no gently. "Please, baby," the boss whispered to her. Gorman had never spoken to her in this gentle tone. She turned to Darius with tears in her eyes. He nodded yes, and she slumped down in the chair, silent.

We moved on to disk 3 and worked quickly to finish. Hours had passed and we were all getting very tired. We covered everything in all 3 disks.

"Now what?", I quizzed. "That's it. That's everything? What do we do with the disks? Destroy them?"

Every single person in the room said in unison, "NO!"

"We keep ours? Trent, you take yours? It really doesn't matter now. There are no more secrets. No more war. It's over."

Trent Winter stood up and approached me. He stroked my face lightly with his fingertips. "You are the keeper of all the disks now, baby. You hold them as the true owner. Just promise me I can have access any time I need them." He lingered a moment, my face in his hand. He winked at me and turned to Sal, who was still blocking the door. "That's it. We go home." Aguzzi packed up all of the notes and grabbed the briefcase.

As they started to leave, I called out behind them, "Winter, is our truce still good?" Trent grinned. He had one more shot at a dig for Gorman. He took my hand and kissed it seductively. "The truce holds." He glared at the ring on my finger coldly. "Nice ring," he scowled, looking me harshly in the eyes. He dropped my hand with a sneer on his lips.

I sighed with relief as they walked out of the door. A huge weight was finally off my shoulders. We were free. Finally free from the war. Now, we could go home. Billy stood next to me. He grabbed my cast and read Trent Winter's message to me. "God, I hate that man," he growled.

Disks in hand, we were on the plane flying back to Las Vegas. Darius and Billy were going over the notes that they had taken. I closed my eyes and sat back in the seat. We weren't in the air long, when Jolene got up and moved into the seat directly across from Billy, staring at him eye to eye. "Now, we talk, Gorman," she demanded. "Was that disk correct? Did you murder Jasmine's mother? And under my father's orders?"

Barrington stiffened, "Jolene," he condemned harshly.

Gorman held his hand up to silence Darius. I was suddenly wide awake, ears open, but I kept my eyes closed, pretending to be sleeping.

Jolene's face was chiseled. She highly expected some sort of groveling or blatant denial. To her surprise and shock, Gorman sat forward in his seat confrontationally. "Jasmine knows what happened and I've forbidden her from discussing the details, Jolene. That was a long time ago. I didn't know any of you then. I can't change the past, but I can change the future." He sat closer to her, inches from her face, his features going hard and cold. "Understand this: I've risked everything to help you two. My organization, my business, and even my life. If it wasn't for me and Barrington, you two would've been tortured and dead by now at the hands of Ken Parks. We are not EVER going to talk about this again."

She shrunk back in her seat timidly. The boss's eyes flashed with ire. The plane went totally silent, and stayed that way for the duration of the flight.

CHAPTER 17

A couple of very quiet months passed after the peace agreement was reached. It was awesome; no longer obsessed with nightmares and the shadows of the past, I could breathe again.

Billy and Darius decided to do a little renovation of the casino. They had been inspired by our trip to Maine and wanted to give the casino a wilderness feel. They created a moving stream with live fish, real trees and vegetation, and even added some animal life from a taxidermist. Gorman moved the Kodiak bear into the center of the casino, and it was an amazing center piece.

One morning we sat over our breakfast and sipped coffee before the guys went to work. The men were reading the morning paper, while Jolene and I thumbed through a book of baby names. She was really starting to show in her pregnancy, and we were so excited.

Suddenly, there was a blood curdling scream from the other room, from Roderick. Billy and Darius looked at each other over the top of the newspaper. They both broke out in laughter. Roderick shouted, "Damn it, Gorman!"

I leapt to my feet and went rushing into the foyer to see what was happening. Calling out, "Roderick! Roderick, what's wrong?" Did no one have the sense to help him in his outburst of terror? As I rounded the corner on a full run, I saw it and stopped dead in my tracks.

A full-sized taxidermy moose with a huge rack of antlers was smack dab in the center of the foyer. It was humongous and majestic. Roderick stood, holding his chest, face pale and a bead of sweat running down his face. "Your boyfriend is an asshole," he grumbled, stomping away angrily.

I returned to the kitchen to find Billy and Darius laughing hysterically. "That wasn't nice," I chastised. "You know how much that moose in Maine scared him."

"Like a little girl," Barrington chuckled. I smiled at the thought of his screaming and running, hiding in the bathroom. "We're having it moved to the casino today. We just had to rib him one more time."

Billy grinned, "I bet he messed his pants."

I sighed, "You better hope he doesn't decide to get even with you two."

Jolene asked, "Can we come in and see the renovations today?"

"Sure," Darius agreed. "We better get going, Billy. The movers should be here any time to load the moose and take it over to the casino."

Later that day, Jolene and I toured the casino and saw all of the changes. The Diamond Eagle felt so much like home now. It was comforting. As we strolled about the casino floor and admiring all that they had done, Billy approached us.

"Girls, I need to talk to you in my office. Follow me." He seemed a little worked up. I rolled my eyes at my sister behind his back. Ok, here we go. Another ass chewing for some violation of an obscure rule we hadn't known about.

Jolene dragged her feet, not wanting to take part in the fall out. We trudged behind slowly, the boss leading us to his private office.

"Girls, take a seat please," Barrington stated.

Jolene whined, "Ok, what did we do wrong now?"

Billy sat down behind the desk. He waived his hand for us to sit and we plopped down in the two chairs facing him. "I need your help," Gorman said softly. We glanced at each other in confusion. "It seems that the casino has received numerous requests lately for weddings to be done here. People want to use our new wilderness theme as a backdrop. Well, we have never had weddings here before. You two girls did such a fantastic job at Jolene and Darius's wedding, I wondered if you would be willing to help me get this project off of the ground? You'll have full control and complete cooperation from the entire staff and management team. Anything you need to make this work. What do you say?"

"That would be great," Jolene flooded, "We could come to work with you guys every day instead of just sitting around the house. Jasmine, are you in with me?"

"Yeah," I smiled, "Let's do it. It will be fun."

Gorman slid a folder across the desk at us. "Great. This is a list of names and contact information on each couple. Take the lead." This was the second time that the boss had needed us to take the lead. I finally felt like we belonged here.

CHAPTER 18

Jolene and I took off running with the wedding planning and in two months we were booking several a week. The renovations were completed, and we had gotten into a good rhythm. My relationship with Billy had also evolved into something magical. The anger management classes were really starting to pay off. The stress of the war was over. Jolene was weeks away from becoming a new mother. I had never seen Barrington so happy.

With the anticipation of a new baby and a new life free from war, we were able to feel innocent again. We had desired this for so long. Hope was renewed and abundant. This child was going to bring joy and purity to our lives.

One afternoon, the boss called Jolene and me into a meeting. As we entered his private office, we were sure that it was to go over the wedding financials. But when we sat down in the chairs facing him, his eyes told a different story. Barrington closed the door and sat down in a third chair. Billy had a perturbed look on his face. "Tell them," Darius said sternly.

Billy sighed, "I just got a call from Trent Winter. He says he needs to take another look at the disks, Jasmine, and he wants to come here to do it. He told me that it would be just him and Salvatore. They want to see the disks and then spend some time gambling in the casino. They called to ask for permission, and I want to know what you think of that."

"I don't like it," Barrington snarled. "I can't stand the idea of them anywhere near the girls or our casino. I don't want them in our city! I don't give a damn how much money they want to spend in the casino. I haven't forgotten what they have done to you girls in the past. He can blame Ken Parks all he wants to, but I don't buy it."

I groaned, "I know, Darius, but to keep the peace agreement, I don't think we have any other choice. We agreed to let him have access to the disks any time he wanted it."

"We already showed him," Barrington said.

"She has a point," the boss added. "If we deny him access to the disks, we are breaking the peace agreement and jeopardizing the treaty."

Darius slumped back in his seat, "Up to Jasmine. I'm just letting you know how I feel."

"Jasmine, keeper of the disks?", Billy mocked.

I tipped my head back and closed my eyes. This really sucked. "I don't think we have a choice," I sighed.

The boss looked about the room at the unhappy faces and moaned, "I'll call him and tell him he can come. Him and Aguzzi only. No other men. We'll keep him under full guard the entire time he is here."

Our meeting was adjourned, and we all dispersed back to our duties at the casino.

A few days later, Trent Winter and Sal Aguzzi walked through the front doors of the Diamond Eagle with all eyes fixed on them. Security immediately engulfed them. We took them to a conference room where Billy had the computers all set up for them and ready to go.

Once again, we went through each disk as Winter took notes feverishly in a small black notebook. It went very fast. "Thank you, Jasmine," Trent announced. "Now, I think we will gamble for awhile before heading back to New York. The work here is done."

Their luck wasn't so good on the casino floor, and they did drop a bundle of cash. I was quick to have the disks locked up in Gorman's private safe and get them out of my possession.

Jolene was indulging in an ice cream sundae with a side of dill pickles when I walked by her at the casino bar. I laughed at her weird food combinations. I gazed out across the busy casino floor and caught sight of Winter at a poker table. The table was surrounded by our men watching their every move.

I shook my head from side to side and made my way to the lady's room. I stood in front of the mirrors, staring at my reflection. So much pain. So much strife. It had been such a long, hard road the last 2 years. Now here we were – a time of peace and cooperation. It had been a long and costly battle, with losses on both sides. All started by that vile and evil bastard Ken Parks. My soul was finally free.

I turned to leave and was startled to see Trent Winter standing there in the bathroom between me and the exit. I was instantly nervous and began formulating an escape plan in my head. I wanted to step around him and run but couldn't get to the door. "What do you want?", I asked.

"You know, Jasmine, our peace treaty is so fragile," he said softly, snaring my wrist. He raised my hand and touched the engagement ring on my finger. He rubbed it gently and spun it around my finger, a look of disdain in his eyes. "One wrong word, one wrong move, and this bliss will be all over." There was no mistaking the threatening tone to his words. I froze in terror, unable to speak up to him. My heartbeat was pounding in my temples.

His cold eyes met mine and held me fast. "You and I have unfinished business, Jasmine." I gulped as he continued to play with the ring on my finger. "So very fragile," he repeated tenderly. He kissed the back of my hand, eyes locking on me intently.

"If this very, very fragile agreement should be broken, I want you to know this:" he paused and his face went icy cold, "I'm coming for you, Jasmine, and this time I'm not returning you to Gorman. You're mine."

He turned and walked toward the door. My knees went weak, and I spoke, "You don't need me anymore, Winter, you have the information from the disks." My whole body was trembling.

He smiled, an evil smile and sneered, "What the hell do you know about what I need, Jasmine?" His voice was sharp and cruel, slashing at my very psyche. He stepped through the door, and I went numb, nearly collapsing to the floor.

The door slowly opened, and my heart was beating fast as Jolene casually strolled inside. "Oh, hi sis," she laughed. "Being pregnant, I gotta go all of the time. Hey, I just saw Winter in the hallway, and he looked pissed. He must be mad at all of the money they lost, right?" I was silent. Jolene narrowed her eyes at me curiously. "Jasmine, what's wrong with your face? You look like you've just seen a ghost."

ABOUT THE AUTHOR

Brenda Bacon was born and raised in the small town of Freeport, Maine: a quaint small town on the beautiful rocky coastline. Her love of writing came at an early age, due to the inspiration and guidance of a very caring English teacher.

She has a deep love and connection for the fabulous city of Las Vegas. There has always been an air of intrigue and excitement surrounding the pulse of the city. It has a calming and spiritual sensation that vibes from the majestic mountains range that looks down upon the city.

Her writing style is of the 1st person, bringing the reader directly into the story. They become Jasmine and see the events unfold through her eyes, thus taking them along each and every wild turn along the way.